Ranjit Lal is the author of over thirty-five books—fiction and non-fiction—for children and adults who are children. His abiding interest in natural history, birds, animals and insects is reflected in many of his books: *The Little Ninja Sparrows, Owlet, Not Out, The Crow Chronicles, The Life and Times of Altu Faltu, The Small Tigers of Shergarh, The Birds of Delhi, The Tigers of Taboo Valley* and others. His other books with social themes include *Faces in the Water, Our Nana Was a Nutcase, Taklu and Shroom, Miracles, Smitten, The Secret of Falcon Heights, The Dugong and the Barracudas* and *The Battle for No. 19*. He enjoys photography, reading and cooking. He lives in Delhi.

The
Hidden Palace
Adventure

A ~~Hate~~ Story — *LOVE*

RANJIT LAL

talking
CUB
An Imprint of Speaking Tiger

TALKING CUB
Published by Speaking Tiger Publishing Pvt. Ltd
4381/4, Ansari Road, Daryaganj
New Delhi 110002

First published in Talking Cub by Speaking Tiger in 2019

ISBN: 978-93-88874-75-5
eISBN: 978-93-88874-74-8

10 9 8 7 6 5 4 3 2 1

The moral right of the author has been asserted.

Typeset in Adobe Garamond Pro by Jojy Philip

The Hidden Palace Adventure

PROLOGUE

'Shh!' the boy warned the girl crouched beside him, putting his finger to her lips. 'We've just entered hostile territory. We must be very quiet!' He was a tall, swarthy teenager with intense black eyes and curly hair.

'Wow!' the girl whispered, her brown eyes wide. 'It's very quiet—do you think anyone's at home?'

'Who knows, they might even have us in their gun-sights!'

'Don't say such things!'

'Well, you read the board: it said, "Intruders shall be gundown".'

'They're just trying to scare people off. They can't gun-down anyone.'

'They're royalty, they think they can do anything.'

Around them, the twisted keekar plants whispered conspiratorially in the breeze. The two youngsters seemed to be the only humans in the entire forest. The girl smiled.

'Yes, I guess they might think that way,' she said, 'this is an old hunting lodge after all. Did you know it's called Malcha Mahal? It was built by Feroze Shah Tughlaq around seven hundred years ago.' But the boy had stopped listening. He suddenly grabbed her hand.

'Did you hear that?'

'What? Don't try to scare me!'

'No! I swear I heard the clanking of chains. You know, like the manacles they use for criminals and cutthroats.'

'You're just trying to scare me—and want to hold my hand! But it's okay, I don't mind.'

'You don't mind what? Being scared or holding my hand?'

The girl smiled prettily. 'Both I suppose, you idiot.'

'Okay, no problem.' The boy grinned, looking at her. Her brown hair was almost golden in the sunlight that was slanting through the trees and her lovely eyes were sparkling. 'If your family knew where we were…' he went on.

'Don't say that. They'd really "gundown" us.' The girl giggled.

Suddenly they stiffened. The clanking of heavy chains could be heard clearly now. Then all hell broke loose as it seemed that the hounds of Hades had started baying simultaneously for their blood.

'Oh shoot,' the boy squawked. 'They've scented us.'

'They'll tear us limb from limb!'

Over the barking, a voice shouted, 'You there. You're trespassing. You have thirty seconds to leave before I fire and let the dogs loose. Now go!'

'Bet he's bluffing,' the boy said with sudden spirit. 'They wouldn't dare shoot us.'

'Bhaiyya would certainly shoot us if he caught us together like this,' the girl said and giggled again. Her soft hand crept into his and clutched it.

The sound of clanking chains grew louder and suddenly the baying barks seemed closer too.

'I think the dogs are after us.'

'Hutt, hutt, shoo-shoo!' the voice shouted above the din of the dogs' barking.

'Run!' the boy yelped.

But already it seemed too late for that. Heavy animal bodies were crashing towards them through the dense undergrowth accompanied by encouraging shouts.

Frozen, the two youngsters—the boy about sixteen and the girl maybe fourteen—clutched each other, unable to move.

Fearfully they peered down the trail as the hunt closed in. The girl turned her face up towards the boy who was looking down at her.

'I love you,' they both squeaked simultaneously; then their eyes widened.

'Chup! Quiet!' the same voice suddenly commanded

and miraculously the barking ceased as did the sounds of the pursuit. They heard the chains clank again, the sound receding and then the forest's secret silence enveloped them once more.

They had no idea how it happened or which one of them made the first move. But long, lingering blissful moments later when their fierce, very first kiss had ended, they drew back, more stunned than they had been than when the dogs had started baying.

'Oh my god!' the girl whispered again, 'What have we done?'

The boy looked even more dazed. There was only the whispery silence of the forest around them again. The girl smiled and linked her arms around his neck and turned her face up to his.

'I don't mind doing it again but afterwards I think we better find our way home before Bhaiyya and Papa start looking for and "gundown" us,' she said.

'Here you go, my dear,' Khushboo said, smiling at me, as she handed me a thick book called *Kidnapped* by some Robert Louis Stevenson fellow. 'I'm sure you'll enjoy this. It's a historical adventure story set in Scotland. You read this while I teach your sister.'

'Thank you,' I mumbled, going a bit red, because Khushboo was very beautiful—anyone could see that—and always smelt so nice. She reminded me of Lavina. Like Khushboo, Lavina had long soft brown hair (I know because it once brushed my cheek) which was like silk, and she was fair and had light brown eyes too. Of course Anshu, my elder sister, who took History and English and Maths tuition from Khushboo said they both were 'a bit plump—like silk cushions'. Khushboo had finished school when she was just sixteen years old, can you imagine, and had come first in entire Delhi or something like that in her Board exams. Then she had studied in one of Delhi's best colleges. They said she was a prodigy—a very, very clever person with the IQ of a rocket scientist. But her family didn't believe in girls making a career and she was now stuck at home. They wanted to get her married as quickly as possible to some very rich man with his own business jet. Lucky person, whoever that would be. She now gave tuitions to kids like Anshu, my sister, who was in the tenth standard.

I sat down on the sofa in the drawing room and started the book. It seemed to be a scary story that started with this dude called Davie Balfour who was an orphan and who had come to stay with his uncle, a cruel old man called Ebenezer Balfour. One day his uncle sent him up a broken, unfinished staircase to the top of a tower in the pitch dark to fetch a chest. The stairs of the tower ended in mid-air and the boy would have fallen and died, which was what the uncle wanted. All this happened on a cold, foggy and thundery night—much like it was outside at the time.

We were not in Scotland, though, but good old Delhi. It was November and the fogs and mists had already begun. I had come along with Anshu because Mama and Papa were at work and Mama had refused to let me be alone at home. She said it was because I had once by mistake put an egg in the microwave. I was thirteen going on fourteen and Mama treated me as if I were seven! Anshu was sixteen, though she behaved like she was twenty-five.

Anyway, that evening I started reading the book, but soon began to listen to what Khushboo was telling Anshu at the dining table. For a change, Anshu was listening to her with rapt attention and not rolling her eyes. I know it's not nice to listen when other people are talking, but I couldn't help it and Khushboo has such a clear and gentle voice that carried over easily from the dining room.

'Yes, the grand but eccentric lady then came to Delhi with her son and daughter, twelve ferocious hounds and five servants, and just camped in the waiting room at New Delhi Railway Station, demanding that the government give her a place to live in accordance with her stature! She was the great great-granddaughter of the last Nawab of Awadh, Wajid Ali Shah and called herself Begum Wilayat Mahal of Awadh. Her ancestors had lived in grand palaces and had huge lands. The British turned them out of their palaces back in 1856 and made her family poor and homeless. The Nawab and his entire court was exiled to Calcutta, where he lived on a pension given by the British. A year later, when the Rebellion of 1857 broke out, he was imprisoned in Fort William. Wajid Ali Shah died in 1887, much to the relief of the British. Begum Wilayat Mahal claimed to be a great great-granddaughter of the

Nawab, and more than a hundred years after the events, demanded compensation from the government for the lands seized by the British. The Begum demanded a fitting place to live from the government. She and her children and dogs landed up in Delhi to press their demand. They lived in the waiting room of New Delhi Railway Station for nine or ten years, before the government, led by Prime Minister Rajiv Gandhi, finally gave them a "palace" in 1985. It was actually an old hunting lodge built by Feroze Shah Tughlaq nearly seven hundred years ago, on what is now the Delhi Ridge. It was called Malcha Mahal, though it had no electricity or running water—or anything—just snakes and scorpions.'

Anshu leaned forward all agog and my ears pricked up too.

'Didi, you mean our Ridge? Where we bike, just across the main road?' Her eyes widened.

Khushboo smiled at her. 'Yes, the very same: you take the Bistadari road off Sardar Patel Marg and head inside the forest...'

'But we cycle in the Ridge very often and have never come across such a Mahal!'

This was true. We just had to cross a busy road and there it was: this great rustling thorny forest. Before you say, 'Hah, don't bluff, you wouldn't have been allowed to cycle there because only criminals go there', let me tell you that our parents of course don't know any of this and anyway we have the 'Six Pack' guarding us.

The Six Pack is our own six 'ferocious hounds' led by Dada, who I think is a mixed breed German shepherd. He is huge, jet black and very hairy and looks just like a wolf. I think he may be part-wolf too, considering how easily he keeps up with us on our cycling trips. He and his partner, Badi-Dadi, lead the pack in just the same way as a wolf pack does: all the other dogs—Loafer, Bomber, Badmash and Lady-Bouncer—have to listen to them or get their ears nipped. The other dogs in the pack are also pariahs and all of them were at one time or the other rescued when they were puppies by the kids in our block, especially Anshu, who's crazy about dogs. They don't live in our houses of course, but in the gardens and common areas and basement where cars and scooters are parked. Our families feed and take care of them and make sure they get their injections.

The Six Pack come with us everywhere we go, especially on our cycling trips to the Ridge. Once some boys on motorcycles tried to whistle at Anshu while we waited for the school bus and the Pack got after them— even making one motorcycle fall! The police were very happy because these guys had been troubling girls for a long time. By around 3 o'clock in the afternoon, the whole pack assembles at the bus-stop where our school bus drops us and escorts us home so our parents don't have to come to receive us. After this started happening, our parents never objected to anything the Six Pack did, and in fact even bought them bedding and coats for winter.

'Dear, the Ridge is an enormous wild jungle!' Khushboo was now telling Anshu. 'People live in Delhi all their lives and still never end up going there. Anyhow, the Begum and her family and dogs settled down there, and soon made it clear that they did not like visitors.' I stole a glance at the dining table. Khushboo was smiling. 'You know, when I was about your age, me and a…err…friend went off there once to explore.' For some reason her cheeks turned pink. Then she continued, 'We knew about the family so approached the place cautiously. The Begum had put up big notices saying, "Entry Restricted. Cautious of Hound Dogs! Visitors will be gundown!" or something to that effect. We were adventurous so we sneaked in. Suddenly we heard the clanking of heavy chains and shackles and then the dogs began barking. They had deep, frightening baying barks, and then someone started shouting that they'd let loose the dogs and shoot us if we didn't run away! By then we were so petrified we couldn't move. We just froze!'

'Oh my god, what happened then?' Anshu asked all agog. 'Didi, what dogs were they?'

'We did not wait around to see them! Actually, I think they were called off because they suddenly stopped barking and we never saw them. But there's a picture of the Begum with what looks like a mastiff, and another in which her son and daughter seem to be with Great Danes, and some newspaper people said she had bloodhounds and Dobermans and even Labradors!'

Anshu shook her head in disbelief. 'We live next door and never knew a thing!'

Khushboo went on with her story: 'The poor Begum was a very unhappy and bitter soul. She committed suicide, it is said, by swallowing crushed diamonds. Then her daughter, Princess Sakina, died and just recently her son, Prince Ali Raza, was found dead on a bed in the Mahal. The family had isolated themselves from everyone, thinking they were above ordinary people. So they died very lonely and unhappy people, who believed they had been wrongly treated by society. I think Malcha Mahal was ransacked after the prince died and few people go there anymore. It is even said to be haunted and full of bats and lizards and snakes!'

'Oh,' Anshu said softly, her black eyes shining and I knew immediately what she was plotting. Today was Saturday, tomorrow willy-nilly (I love that term) we would be out cycling in the Ridge to the haunted Malcha Mahal. My sister was like that only. All the other members of our cycling gang—Lavina, Shiv, Pankaj and Nasreen—follow her blindly. I have no choice because I don't want to be left behind. I only hoped that Anshu would choose to go in the afternoon, because in the morning Shiv and I had cricket coaching with Salim who also lived in our block. He says I could become a 'thunderbolt' fast bowler. He had played for Delhi and had once even substituted in an International Test Match. But then he said he wanted to study medicine, so he gave it up. Now, while he is still a student, he coaches Shiv and me and some other boys in the neighbourhood. He's tall and thin and dark brown with black eyes that can pierce right through a batsman. He told me that though I was not too strongly built, I ran very fast 'like a ferret' and could bowl much quicker than what batsmen would expect from a bowler my size.

'So nobody lives in the Mahal now?' Anshu asked Khushboo, her eyebrows rising questioningly.

'I don't think so. I heard it was ransacked. Such a tragic ending really.'

'Hmm…' Anshu answered and I knew she would now go all broody and thoughtful.

Just then the doorbell rang and Khushboo went to open the door. It was her elder brother Vineet and another person I didn't know. Both had motorcycle helmets in their hands. They were wearing T-shirts and jeans and you could see the muscles bulging out of their arms—they looked like wrestlers. Vineet was about six foot tall and had short hair and hadn't shaved for some days; his friend was a little shorter, but broader, with long, greasy hair and a scruffy beard that made him look dangerous—not the kind of person you would like to meet at night in a dark alley. He wore a thick gold bracelet and a huge watch. His eyes glittered and flickered around everywhere. I saw him stare at Khushboo and raise his eyebrows and smile. He looked even more dangerous when he did that—like he was baring his teeth in a sneer.

'Tea!' Vineet demanded brusquely, 'Khushboo, get us tea and some samosas.' Then he realized that a class was in progress and shook his head as if exasperated.

'I'll bring it to your room,' Khushboo said in a level voice, but her face had suddenly all closed up like those touch-me-not mimosa leaves. 'I have class, as you can see.'

'Doesn't matter what you have; you serve it to us anyway right now,' her brother snapped. 'Biker can stay for only a short while.'

'Ji, Bhaiyya!' Khushboo said in a flat tone. Just then Khushboo's maroon mobile, which was lying on the dining table warbled. Before she could pick it up, Vineet strode up and snatched it.

'Yes?' he asked brusquely. His face convulsed in

anger and he flung the phone against the wall as hard as he could. It shattered into pieces.

'He is still calling you,' he snarled and as we looked on, appalled, he grabbed her long hair. She just stared back at him defiantly, her cheeks going red.

'The next time this happens…' he grated, 'the next time…'

'Bhaiyya, please!' Anshu stuttered, horrified.

Biker just stood there with his arms crossed, watching and nodding slightly, a smirk on his face. Vineet suddenly realized that he had an audience and let go. He stomped off with Biker, deliberately crunching the pieces of Didi's shattered phone on the floor. As they walked away, I saw Biker stare at Anshu who was flipping through her notebook. Then he disappeared into the room.

'Sorry about that, children,' Khushboo said, settling her hair and pursing her lips. 'As you saw, Vineet has a rather nasty temper. Okay Anshu, I think we'll call it a day,'

'Okay, Didi. Thank you,' Anshu said. 'I'll read this and return the book next time. The Ridge story was fascinating!'

'Umm…Anshu, on Wednesday will it be all right if I come to your house for the tuition?' Khushboo asked.

'Sure thing, Didi!'

I put *Kidnapped* on the dining table. 'Thank you, Didi,' I said and she smiled and handed the book back to me. 'You keep it until you finish it. As I was telling your sister, the best way to improve your English is by reading as much as you can.'

We said goodbye and left quickly, shaken by what we had seen. There was a steely look in Anshu's eyes as we made our way back home. Suddenly she grabbed my hand.

'Listen, we tell no one about what happened. Got it?' she said. I nodded quickly.

'Sure,' I mumbled. Then I glanced at her. 'What about the Ridge thing, though?'

She gave a wry smile. 'That's okay, we're going to tell everyone about that.' She gave me a sudden hug.

'You know, if you had been even a tiny bit like that Vineet, I would have had to murder you.'

Anshu was on the phone talking to Lavina the moment we got home.

'Listen Lav,' she said, 'you won't believe this!'

Within fifteen minutes she had organized everything. Tomorrow afternoon at 3.30 we would set out into the Ridge on our cycles and find the haunted Malcha Mahal. The entire gang would be coming.

This is a good place to introduce our cycling 'gang'.

Anshu, my sister, is easily the leader even though Shiv sometimes pretends that he is boss, until Anshu tells him, 'Shut up, Goofball, and sit tight.' Then he grins and shrugs as if to say, 'What to do with a girl like that?' But I think he secretly admires Anshu for this. Anshu's very keen on playing the guitar and is pretty good at it (her heroine is Gabriella Quevedo), though she wasn't all that pleased when Mama and Papa gave her a lovely dark blue hand-made guitar for her birthday instead of the smartphone she had been hoping for. Anshu doesn't realize it but she relies on me for advice when we get into 'situations', which usually means trouble.

Shiv is a good sportsman and spends as much time as he can outdoors messing about with the Six Pack in the parking lot for hours at a time. His dad died when he was a baby and his mum has brought him up all on her own. She runs a successful business and he always goes on about how girls are as good, if not better than guys, which is why Anshu is probably his best friend.

Privately, I think Anshu likes Shiv very much indeed, probably because they both are crazy about the dogs (who never listen to them) and he never takes offence to her teasing.

Pankaj, with his round face and 'matching' round spectacles is twelve and bit of a nerdy weirdo—more interested in creepy crawlies like ants and spiders and cockroaches than people. He secretly writes poems and spends a lot of time just staring at the ground or at a plant or the grass. He has a thing for spiders especially, and had once told Nasreen that her eyes were just like those of a jumping spider's. Nasreen rapped him one smartly on the back of his head and retorted, 'Oh yeah? Be careful of what you say or I'll eat you!' but when he actually showed her a jumping spider, her eyes widened and she exclaimed, 'Oh but their eyes are so bright and beautiful! They are gorgeous!' Pankaj went bright pink and I bet he'd begun making up a poem about how ferocious lady spiders eat their boyfriends after stunning them with their gorgeous eyes. He's also our gang's photographer and never travels without his black 24X Lumix.

Nasreen is slim as a reed with 'shining black olive' eyes (that's Pankaj again, and why I suspect he scribbles poetry about her). She can put two fingers in her mouth and whistle like a hoodlum. The dogs always listen to her much more than they do to the rest of us. She has this deep, husky voice that according to Pankaj sounds like 'a golden wheat-field rustling in the wind' and can hold us spellbound when she sings.

Lavina is fifteen going on sixteen, and quite like Khushboo—fair and with light brown eyes and a bit cushiony, but as Anshu once cattily said 'minus the brains'. She says she wants to be a heart surgeon and happily patches and plasters us up after our rides through the thorny trees in the Ridge. I love it when she does this because she has such soft hands and a gentle touch and sweet smile. But she's a solid long-distance cyclist too. I love to watch her pedalling with her ginger-brown hair streaming behind her as she bends over the handlebars or simply sits upright and pedals steadily on, hands-free. She says she is a hotchpotch, 'fruit-salad' kid because her parents and grandparents came from all over the place—both from India and outside.

As for me, I'm Umesh, almost fourteen and I like to think the brainiest and sharpest of the bunch. I love figuring out why things happen—detecting and analyzing events and issues threadbare. I'm compactly built and as I said earlier, I would like to be a 'thunderbolt' fast bowler.

All of us love cycling—especially 'off-road' cycling—and we take very good care of our bikes. 'Lulu Cycle Mart' down the road gives us great discounts on repairs and maintenance. All our bikes have tough, knobbly 'all-terrain' tyres, independent suspension and gears and caliper brakes as well as lights and carrier bags, speedometers and odometers. Salim has also taught us basic maintenance skills—how to oil and clean the bikes properly, especially after muddy rides in the rain. We really love exploring the narrow bumpy trails inside the central Delhi Ridge. Most of the trees here are (according to Pankaj) 'vilayati' keekar and babul—very thorny and spiky—and have caused innumerable punctures. We always carry puncture-repair kits and tyre-pumps. Most of these trees are not very big, but look (as Anshu once said) like 'dried up, with contorted arms and legs beseeching us to get caught in their embrace' so they could tear us to shreds and 'bleed us dry'. In some places the paths on the Ridge are so narrow and rocky and blocked with thorny bushes and rocks that we have to carry our bikes through or over them.

'This is going to be so exciting,' Anshu told Shiv who had quickly turned up to listen to the whole story. 'Imagine, we'll be in a palace where an actual maharani and prince and princess lived in exile for so many years! We've been such idiots to not have discovered it earlier.'

Then she looked at me speculatively. 'Are you sure you'd like to come?' she asked. 'It could be scary. Besides, Mama and Papa will be home tomorrow, so you could easily stay behind.'

'Of course I want to come,' I said indignantly.

Anshu frowned and looked skeptical. 'I really don't think you should,' she said shaking her head. 'You're just a bachcha! You'll freak out. Besides, it will be a long ride.'

'You'll freak out!' I replied shrilly, but now getting seriously worried that I might indeed be left behind. I narrowed my eyes and deployed my ultimate weapon of deterrence.

'If you don't let me come along, I'll tell Mama where you all are going!'

'You know, you're such a little weirdo and so easy to tease,' Anshu said, suddenly all smiles. She came up to me and hugged me. 'Sure you can come along, baba,' she said pinching my cheek. 'Provided you promise not to whine that you're tired and want to go back.' Anshu was like that, what to do? She'd spend the whole day teasing me wretchedly and then suddenly give me a huge hug and big smacking kisses and say, 'Idiot! I love you so much, I wonder why!' Weird, but what to do?

But of course, I had to go along. We'd be going to a haunted old palace. What if one of us were to get caught in a thorn-bush or in a poisonous spider's web? Or worse, what if the embittered ghosts of the Begum and her children—and their dogs—showed up?

2

Shiv and I met in our block's park for cricket coaching at 10 a.m. the next morning. Being November, the weather was pleasant all through the day so there was no need to get up very early in the morning for coaching. Salim hadn't as yet joined us but we knew the drill and began warming up: doing exercises and then running around the park. He turned up in about fifteen minutes and put up the wickets in the nets. Our parents, though they were hardly around to watch our matches, had pooled in to buy us a proper net to practice in.

'It's not that they think you're going to be the next Virat Kohli or Tendulkar or Dale Steyn or Mitchell or whoever,' Anshu had cattily told Shiv and me, grinning. 'It's just that they don't want any more windows broken.'

'Yeah, yeah, whatever,' Shiv nodded. But the net did make us take our cricket more seriously, and it did, I think, impress others. This morning for instance, we were well into our coaching session when two bikes drew up raucously at the far end. The bikers got off to watch. To my surprise, I realized they were Vineet and his friend Biker. Great, I thought, walking up to the end of my bowling run, as Shiv took guard. Let's show these pehelwans!

Salim briefly glanced at the bikers and then came up to me. 'Okay, three whistlers—perfume balls and then the yorker—let's see how Shiv handles them.'

'Sure, sir.'

I let loose three ferocious bouncers, all of which Shiv easily weaved away from. But he was stepping away a bit. Then I hurled down the toe-crunching yorker but the bugger was ready for it. He just bounced down the track and smacked it on the full straight past me.

'Well played!' Salim cheered. The ball streaked past me and stopped near the watching bikers. Salim ran up to pick it up. When he reached, he found Vineet standing over it, one foot on top of the ball. Salim held out his hand and said something, probably, 'Can you hand me the ball, please?'

Vineet kicked the ball to Biker, who now leered at Salim, inviting him to take it. Suddenly, Vineet stepped up to Salim and seemed to hold him by the collar. He said something and spat viciously in his face. Shiv and my mouths dropped about two feet. Salim stepped back, carefully wiped his face with his handkerchief. But we could see his fists bunching. Vineet (who was taller and more strongly built) took a step forward and violently pushed Salim backwards with both hands. Just then Mukhi Aunty who lives in our block and is nearly 100 years old (and a real nosey parker) came doddering past, smiling benignly.

'Having fun, boys?' she asked. Immediately, Vineet was all smiles.

'Ji, Auntieji!' he said, folding his hands and bending down as if to touch her feet. Salim just nodded and came loping back to us. Vineet and Biker having seen Mukhi Aunty off stared at us for a minute then got on their bikes and roared off.

'Bhai sahib, you'll have to out-think him,' Salim told me, handing me the ball. 'Shiv knows just what to expect from you.' He behaved as though nothing untoward had just happened. And so though Shiv and I were dying to find out what had gone down between Salim and Khushboo's brother, we continued to play and practice till it was time for lunch.

At 3.30, we all gathered in the main parking lot, ready and excited about the expedition to locate Malcha Mahal in the Ridge. Anshu had properly wound up the whole gang telling them that we'd be going to a haunted old palace. (She loves scaring people.) Pankaj and Lavina had looked a little nervous, but not Nasreen and Shiv. I just put my faith in the Six Pack: as long as they were with us I knew we'd be safe. If there were ghosts around they'd sense them and not let us go there or get into any danger. Animals knew these things better than humans.

'Be careful where and how you ride,' Ma told us as usual. 'Take your helmets and don't go out on the main roads.' Luckily, she had not looked out of the windows too carefully or seen the weather forecast. The sky was overcast with a light yellowish-grey cloud cover. It had turned into a murky day and visibility was not too good. The forecast had said that a 'western disturbance' was on its way along with light rain. But that wasn't going to stop us.

Where the paths and roads were wide enough, we biked two abreast: Anshu and Shiv, followed by Nasreen and Pankaj, and myself and Lavina bringing up the rear. The dogs ran by our sides, up and down, panting happily. On narrower paths it had to be single file, with usually either Anshu or Shiv in the lead and me and Lavina bringing up the rear. We biked up Sardar Patel Road using the pavement actually: there weren't many pedestrians walking this afternoon. Then we came to the right turn leading into Bistadari Road and immediately, it got darker and gloomier as the trees crouched over us like a dark green roof. The narrow, empty road snaked mysteriously into the silent forest ahead. Occasionally, small groups of monkeys sitting on the roadside eyed us before quickly disappearing into the trees when they saw the dogs. Partridge and peacocks called from somewhere among the trees, startling us. Anshu, leaning over her handlebars, looked back towards us as we sailed down the road.

'Do you know this whole Ridge forest was planted by the Brits?' she called out. She'd been reading the book Khushboo had given her and was now flaunting her new-found knowledge. 'Apparently they got so roasted and stewed on the Ridge during the 1857 Uprising that they swore it could never happen again and so planted an entire forest to cool the city down.'

'Well, the idiots should have planted less thorny stuff,' Lavina said. 'There's even cactus growing here.'

'Yeah, we'd have less punctures that way!'

'How much further?' Pankaj asked, glancing at his back wheel. His bike was making a rattling sound as a twig or dried leaf was probably caught in the spokes.

'This road leads to the ISRO Satellite Tracking Station but we have to turn off before it. There should be a path to our right. Keep a lookout,' Anshu replied, now sitting up straight on her bike and free-wheeling. After a while she skidded to a halt. 'This looks like it. We turn here and follow this. Okay guys, we're soon entering hostile territory, so keep your eyes and ears open!'

'Yeah, yeah!'

The weather had turned even murkier. The contorted keekars stuck out their branches through the cobweb-grey mist like desiccated stunted limbs. A faint pattering sound started, as if the trees were whispering secretively and a thin gauzy drizzle began to fall. I remembered the scene from *Kidnapped* and shivered. Would we, too, be lured up steps that led into thin air so that we would fall to our deaths? The path went up a small hillock and then was blocked by a thick fallen branch. We dismounted and hauled our bikes over it and wheeled them on. At a short distance, the broken walls of Malcha Mahal loomed up, and then the 'palace' itself was right in front of us. It stood there, silent and empty and hulking, surrounded by twisted cactus plants and thorny bushes. We couldn't find any warning boards. The building had no windows or doors—just arches. The front 'door', which was just a barred iron gate had fallen right over and lay almost flat on the ground.

'Wow!' we exclaimed in hushed whispers as the Six Pack sniffed around excitedly. I wondered if they could catch the long-ago scents left by the 'ferocious hounds'. They didn't seem particularly bothered.

'Come on guys, let's go in,' Anshu said. My sister's eyes were gleaming. She glanced up at the sky through the mesh of branches. 'Looks like it's drizzling. Better take the bikes inside too.'

We hauled our bikes up the steep steps and entered a sunken dungeon-like large room. Khushboo had been right. The place had been ransacked. The only thing left were scraps of paper and torn pages from magazines scattered over the floor, getting blown this way and that. A couple of small glass-fronted cupboards stood open— bare. The walls were dank and mossy and there was a dreadful mouldy smell in the air. We stood together in a close bunch, looking around and up at the dark ceiling.

Then, first one and then another and then many more flapping black shadows detached themselves from the roof with a chittering, screechy sound—bats! This was followed by a heart-stopping 'Bhhrrr!' and a pair of large, flapping birds blundered out. The dogs barked in surprise.

'Eeek!' Lavina shrieked and I suddenly found that she was clinging on to me. Shiv and Pankaj squawked in alarm, 'Hoi! Watch out!' as Nasreen, ever laconic, exclaimed, 'Whoops!'

'Cool it, guys. They're just bats and pigeons but god do they stink!' That, needless to add, was my unflappable sister. As for me, Lavina had virtually smothered the breath out of me as she clutched me tightly around the waist, not that I was complaining or anything. The dogs had let out half-barks of surprise before swirling around our legs wagging their tails.

We regained our composure. Lavina let me go, and

Shiv and Pankaj looked a little sheepish. Nasreen was grinning. We peered around the room. More steep steps led up through another doorway probably to the roof. The dogs milled around our legs, whining softly. Outside, the mist seemed to get thicker, sending wafting entrails through the arches as if in search of necks to wrap themselves around.

'Look,' Anshu said, pointing to a rickety wooden table. 'This must have been the dining table: there were pictures of this with the table laid out with fancy dishes and cups and plates and goblets.' She grinned wickedly and rummaged in her rucksack. 'I've brought some stuff for us to eat; samosas and wafers and popcorn and namkeen,' she said, extracting a sheaf of plates made from leaves (she'd obviously gone shopping that morning) and cups made of clay—the kind you find at railway stations. Lavina too had started rummaging in her rucksack.

'I've brought some gulab jamuns,' she said, smiling happily. 'I just hope the packet hasn't leaked!'

Pankaj and Shiv had been exploring on their own. They'd gone up the steps and returned soon. 'Nothing up there, another barred gate,' they reported.

'Some of the spiders in the corners are just humongous,' Pankaj announced, flashing his pencil torch into the darkness.

'Can you imagine, those people lived here alone

for years with no electricity or running water,' Anshu shook her head. 'All they had were the bats and creepy crawlies and snakes, and mosquitoes, and jackals howling at night, and yet they lived as if they were royalty in a grand palace! They'd even laid down Persian carpets here!'

We lapsed into silence as we tried to imagine what it might have been like. Anshu and Lavina began 'laying the table', which was quite bizarre really. Lavina had brought a bunch of plastic spoons and forks for us to eat our gulab jamuns with, as well as dinky little multi-coloured clear plastic glasses shaped like wine flutes.

'Hey, did you hear that?' Anshu said suddenly, pausing at the table and cocking her head.

'What?' Shiv asked.

'Like a growl…in the distance.'

'Eh? Don't try and scare us!'

'Shh…just listen. Something's beyond those trees, outside. Rumbling…! Now it's stopped.'

'Sure, sure!'

I looked at the gang. Nasreen had a 'been-there, done-that' sort of smile on her face. Shiv was standing arms akimbo and Pankaj seemed to have found something interesting crawling up one wall and hadn't paid attention at all. Lavina was pale and a little wide-eyed. Anshu was still listening with her head cocked to one side the way dogs do. She shook her head.

'Can't hear anything now,' she said. 'But there was something out there.'

That's when Dada and Badi-Dadi began growling softly. The hair on the backs of their necks and down their spines began to rise to form dark ridges. The other dogs drew around them and began growling too, baring their teeth. We looked at each other, our faces pale.

'What?'

'Listen…'

All we could hear was the whispery patter of fine rain and the occasional secretive rustle of leaves chasing each other. Dada and Badi-Dadi faced the doorway through which we had entered. They were beginning to growl a little louder and more angrily now. The back of my neck prickled.

Suddenly voices and raucous laughter emerged out of the gloom: catcalling voices and lewd hyena-like giggles along with the sound of bodies thrashing clumsily through the undergrowth, snapping twigs and tearing leaves. Branches cracked and broke. The dogs' growls deepened. Four figures emerged from the gloom: four unsavoury-looking youths in tight jeans and grubby shirts. They had beer bottles in their hands and were weaving from side to side. They peered myopically through the murk at the hulking 'mahal' in front of them. Then they raised their mobiles to take selfies.

'*Dekho bhoot bangla!*' one shouted, pointing.

'*Mahal hain, yaar, mahal!*' Followed by more laughter.

'The queen's ghost is coming!' another announced grandiosely and they all fell about laughing and shoving each other.

'I'm feeling scared. There must be dogs!'

'Come on, let's go in. We'll show them who's the boss.'

They lurched towards the stone steps.

'Back, back—get inside out of sight, get down, get down,' Anshu hissed, shoving us all back out of sight from the doorway. 'They mustn't see us.' But our bicycles were all lined up in the 'front room' as were the dogs, now growling steadily. The fellows just had to climb up two steps and they'd see them. Anshu glanced at Nasreen and nodded. Nasreen grinned and then lifted her head to the roof and cupped her hands around her mouth.

'Aaaooooo!' she howled eerily, making all of us jump. It echoed horribly around the room.

Immediately the dogs took up the refrain.

They raised their muzzles skywards. 'Aaaaaooooo-oooooo!' they chorused together. 'Aaaaoooooo!' they howled.

Lavina clutched me and squeaked, 'Oh my god!'

The effect on the youths was electric.

'*Arre baap re—kutte ka bhoot!*'

'Look there. Kala kutta! It's like a bear!'

'*Bhaag re bhaag!*'

They turned and fled helter-skelter. We heard them crash through the undergrowth and then in the distance motorbikes started up and roared away. Within minutes, we were surrounded again by silence, broken only by the whispering drizzle that had now got slightly heavier.

Well, after that we had our weird tea-party in Malcha Mahal undisturbed for the rest of the afternoon. It was strange, because after we had eaten and drunk and packed up our things, we just sat around quietly as the dogs curled around us, then lay down and snoozed.

Anshu sat at the edge of the stone steps, staring into the forest and rain and I knew she was trying to imagine what it must have been like to live here.

Shiv, sitting next to her, must have been wondering about the kind of hunts that were organized from here by Feroze Shah Tughlaq.

Nasreen was probably wondering about the Begum and her children and their dogs—the princess Sakina and prince Ali Raza and how tragically they had all died.

Pankaj was still flashing his torch into the corners, disturbing spiders and creepy crawlies as Lavina watched him in horror.

And I watched Lavina almost hypnotized. In the dim silvery light coming through the arches, her face glowed as if lit from inside and her gingery hair looked like it was on fire. She glanced at me and smiled and I felt my cheeks get all hot and red as I quickly looked away. But it was good she knew I was keeping watch over her.

By 5.30 it had begun to get seriously dark and it was time to go back before our parents began pacing about and looking at their watches. None of us had mobile phones: that was another thing our parents had decided we didn't need just yet, despite much protests from us.

'It's simple: if you don't have a phone you won't be able to ring us to tell us that you're going to be late and so you won't be late,' Ma had infuriatingly told Anshu who had tried to lay on the spiel of how we'd be able to inform them about where we were and when to expect us back, every minute of the day, etc. Ma was smart.

The rain had stopped but the gloom had deepened. It was time to be somewhere where the lights were bright. 'Okay guys, time to get back,' Anshu said, breaking the strange spell that seemed to have come over us. 'It's quite a long ride back.'

And then she dropped her bombshell.

'You know, we really must plan to spend a night here sometime. Then we'll really know what it might have been like to live here.'

3

I wasn't too worried about what Anshu had said about spending a night at the haunted Malcha Mahal. It would take a lot of planning. We would all have to give watertight (and false) explanations to our parents, which would have to hold up to scrutiny and cross-examination. But I knew Anshu—she wasn't the kind to give up easily and would be thinking up ways and means. Meanwhile, she had also declared that she would be spending the whole of the coming Sunday at Malcha Mahal, and we could come along if we wanted, but didn't have to. Khushboo had given her an assignment on the place and 'I want to experience what it really must have been like to live there, so I can write it properly,' she told us. Of course we were not about to let her spend the whole day there alone (we really believed in the musketeers' motto of 'One for All and All for One') so the whole gang was going. The Six Pack would accompany us as usual.

'It'll be fun!' Shiv said, his eyes shining. 'And if there are any more unwelcome visitors we know what to do.'

'What if we have to go to the bathroom?' Lavina asked. Anshu looked at her and rolled her eyes.

'Lav, the whole forest is there! If you want, Nas or I can accompany you when you want to go.'

'Thanks!'

I hadn't been able to make too much progress with *Kidnapped* and so was a little worried when I got back from school that Wednesday, fully expecting Khushboo to ask me how I had been progressing. To my surprise and relief I learned that Anshu would be going over to her place. I didn't have to accompany her today because Ma was home. I was watching TV when Anshu got back from her tuition at around 6.30 that evening and to my surprise she came straight up to me.

'Umesh, come here a minute,' she said, beckoning to me. I followed her to her room rather surprised because usually she didn't like anyone in her room. Not that anyone would want to spend too much time in her room anyway: everything was arranged in pin-perfect order, all the books kept in order of height, her desktop neatly covered, multi-coloured cushions arranged perfectly on the bed with her huge stuffed tiger and lion lying on either side. She didn't like a thing out of place.

'When's your next cricket coaching class?' she asked.

'Saturday morning.'

'Okay, give this to Salim then,' she said. She took out a long, plain, brown envelope from her knapsack and gave it to me. 'Just don't lose it, okay?'

'Sure,' I said, turning the envelope over in my hands. Nothing was written on it, and it felt quite heavy but not stiff.

'And don't you dare open it or anything,' Anshu went on, her hands on her hips, her eyes narrowing. 'I'll kill you if you do.'

'Why should I?' I shrugged. 'Sure, I'll give it to Salim, no problem.'

'Good boy,' she said and gave me another of her hugs. 'Now get out of my room!'

'Um...who is it from?' I asked, smirking. 'Who shall I say it is from?'

'That's something you don't need to know or bother yourself with, okay? It's none of your business.'

I shrugged. 'Okay, fine!'

'Go put it in your kitbag right now so you won't forget,' she added.

'Sure, sure, no need to nag!'

I did that but I also nearly forgot to give it to Salim that Saturday. I was stuffing my batting gloves into my bag when I saw the envelope, now slightly worse for wear from lying at the bottom of the bag. I pulled it out and went running after Salim who was walking off towards his Scooty with his bag slung over his shoulder. Shiv had already left and so was not around.

'Salim Bhai!' I yelled, chasing after him and waving the envelope in one hand. 'This is for you. My sister gave it to me to give to you.'

He took the envelope from me and walked slowly to his Scooty.

'Thank you,' he said as I hung around, hoping he would open it. To my delight he did. A whole sheaf of crinkly tissue-like writing paper unfolded. It was obviously a letter—an actual handwritten letter, can you imagine? Salim scanned the pages swiftly, turning them over quickly before folding up the letter again and stuffing it back into the envelope. His face seemed quite blank as if it were neither good news nor bad.

'Okay, I'll be going,' I said. He waved a hand.

'Wait a minute.' He sort of gulped and then rummaged around in his pockets and took out a ballpoint pen. Then he opened his bag and took out a fat notebook and ripped out a page. He sat down on the Scooty and began scribbling. After he'd finished, he folded it up and looked around, frowning.

'You need an envelope?' I asked.

He nodded and then shook his head. 'No, it's okay. I can use this.' He took out the original letter and stuffed the pages into his pocket and put his note in the same brown envelope.

'Oh!' he frowned, looking around. Obviously, he had no glue or cellotape or stapler to seal the envelope with.

'Salim Bhai, you could use a strip of sticking plaster from the first-aid kit,' I said suddenly. I had been given (by Lavina) a small first-aid pouch in my kitbag to patch us up if we got hurt and this included a roll of sticking plaster.

'Good idea,' he said, patting my head. He ripped off a strip of sticking plaster and sealed the envelope.

'Give this to your sister to return to the person who gave it to her, please,' he told me.

'Sure, no problem.'

Anshu nearly freaked when I handed her back the same envelope, creased and battered, now with the sticking plaster strip sealing it.

'What's this?' she yelled, 'You didn't give it to him? And I told you not to open it! I can't believe it! You've patched it up with sticking plaster!'

'Anshu, this is from Salim. He told me to tell you to give it to whoever gave the letter to you,' I cocked my head to one side and raised my eyebrows. Anshu snatched the envelope.

'Oh!' she said. 'Hmm…I see.'

Anshu gave me another (fresh) envelope that Saturday evening with the same instructions as before.

'I won't be coaching with Salim tomorrow,' I said.

'We're going cycling to Malcha Mahal, remember? I'll meet him on Monday and give it to him then.'

She shrugged. 'Okay, no problem.'

By now I had a pretty good idea of what these letters probably were: mushy love letters written by my sister to Salim! She had probably developed a sudden huge crush on him. The only way to confirm this would be to actually open a letter and read it, but I had to summon up the courage to do that. I really didn't mind it if Anshu had a crush on Salim Bhai, even though he was much older than her. He was a good guy: he coached us diligently and quite strictly. But I wondered if he had a crush on Anshu, too. He had never really talked about her to me. Also, I couldn't understand why they couldn't just talk to each other face to face. Maybe one of them was shy! I was so absent-minded that evening that I put the letter she had given me into my knapsack, which I would be taking on our 'full-day expedition' to Malcha Mahal the next day, instead of in my cricket kitbag. But I had made sure that everything else we might need was there: flashlight, compass, energy bars, camera, penknife and even binoculars. Anshu was also smuggling the small portable gas stove, which we kept at home for emergencies, and some packets of noodles.

'We'll cook them there,' she said, her black eyes gleaming, 'Just to see how it tastes and feels.'

We set off at 8 o'clock the next morning. The

western disturbance of the previous week had been followed by another and there had been a record amount of rain. But now it had cleared up, leaving the sky blue and clean, which was unusual for this time of the year. It was a cool misty-sunny morning, with shafts of sunlight angling down through the trees; the tree-trunks were dark brown and looked like chocolate chip. We'd bluffed madly to our parents, telling them that we were going to the Nehru Memorial Museum grounds to spend the day there. The route to that place from where we lived was not at all congested (especially on a Sunday) or too far and we would not have to actually cycle on any busy main road.

'Will they allow the dogs in?' Ma asked doubtfully.

'Ma, if they don't, the dogs can wait outside the gates or in the parking lot,' Anshu had glibly answered. 'They won't be a problem.'

'All right! But be back by around 4 o'clock. It's beginning to get dark early now.'

Where we were really going was almost in the opposite direction!

By around 8.45 a.m. we reached Malcha Mahal—and were in for a huge disappointment. In fact, we knew something was wrong just before we reached the turn-off from Bistadari Road. There were six enormous blue buses parked on one side of the road, with their drivers and cleaners hanging around, smoking bidis and playing cards. As we approached the monument, we heard voices and laughter—and worst of all—loud filmy music blaring out.

'Oh shoot,' Anshu said, stopping and dismounting. 'There must be about 300 people here today.'

A huge group had come here to picnic just like we had. We could hear them whoop and shout and laugh and frankly I felt sorry for the bats.

'Boss, what do we do?' Shiv asked Anshu. 'Do we go ahead?'

She shook her head and shuddered. 'Let's just check; we can't stay here.'

We pushed our bikes over the fallen log and stopped when the monument came into view. There were people swarming all over it. A group of ladies was sitting around a stove attached to a full-sized gas cylinder and cooking. We could smell paranthas frying. Already they had scattered plastic water bottles and plastic bags everywhere. Bulky-looking men in rumpled pullovers were going in and out of the palace, shouting loudly. Kids ran everywhere, occasionally falling over and then bawling. We watched in horror.

'You know what?' Shiv said. 'No ghost is going to haunt this place ever again!'

'Yes,' Anshu said, 'these people have desecrated this place. They have no respect for history.'

Even the Six Pack were nonplussed and just milled

around us, whining questioningly. We had stopped near the apex of a bend and it was only now that I noticed a very narrow trail running due north-east from here seemingly straight into the heart of the forest and diametrically away from Malcha Mahal. I went up to Anshu.

'Maybe we should go down that path?' I suggested. 'We could explore it.'

'What are you talking about? Where?'

I pointed it out. It was a 'single-file' path and even single-file would probably mean we'd have to bash our way through sections where it got even narrower.

'Okay,' Anshu said, throwing up her hands, 'Why not? We might as well. We can't go back home, we've packed stuff for the whole day. And we can't stay here.' She got on her bike and pedalled off down the path. The dogs scampered through the undergrowth and went ahead and then one by one the rest of us followed, clanking and jolting and happily splashing through the many muddy puddles left behind by the rain. I took a quick look at my odometer (I'd got into the habit) before we set forth; it read 240 km, which was what we had clocked in the last couple of months. I was a little annoyed that as usual I was bringing up the rear. I felt I ought to have been up front, leading the pack, because I had been the first to see and discover this path. But hah! Tell that to my bossy sister! Just ahead of me was

Lavina who kept glancing back from time to time as if to check I hadn't got left behind or something. She flashed a smile and I felt my face go red and warm.

'Woohoo, this is great!' I heard Anshu whoop delightedly as we free-wheeled bumpily down a narrow slope. Occasionally the path narrowed so much that the branches of the trees whipped and slashed at our arms and we had to watch out for those diabolical keekar thorns and sometimes duck our heads and shield our eyes. But it was the kind of 'wild' bike ride we just loved. Often we had to dismount and push our bikes through the tangled undergrowth and foliage, keeping a lookout for thorns and wasps. It was our first time on this trail and we had to make our way through it rather like an ice-breaker making its way through pack ice. The second time round would be easier. The dogs kept pace with us easily. We really couldn't ride very fast here. Sometimes they went ahead of us; then at slightly wider sections they would let us pass and follow us, their eyes bright, their grins wide, tongues hanging out. We struggled up a slope and then the path went down quite steeply again, really narrowing at this section. I could hear Shiv and Pankaj and the others chatter and laugh as they biked. I was more focused on what my front wheel was doing and where it was going. We were really deep in the heart of the Ridge and it was impossible to believe that the whole of Delhi surrounded us.

'Eeeek!' Lavina suddenly screamed as she began descending a slope, just behind Nasreen. Then I heard Anshu yell, 'Yikes, watch it!' but I really couldn't see what had happened up ahead. There was a clanging noise, a splash and a shout from Shiv and I knew there had been a collision or something up front—someone had got unseated. Then Lavina jammed on her brakes and skidded, her front wheel turning at right angles and plunging into the undergrowth. It was all she could do not to fall right over. I ran right into her from behind, unable to stop in time. She had just managed to dismount when she saw me teetering straight into her. She dropped her bike and caught me and we staggered back and fell into the spiky undergrowth, with me right on top of her. I felt I had fallen on a lovely soft cushion.

'Ooof!' she snorted and giggled, her face suddenly flush against mine. Her soft cheek squished against my burning one and I felt her arms hold me to her. 'Are you okay? You really are a cutie!' she murmured. Then she smiled and gently pushed me away. 'Now get off me, baba!' When we got to our feet we saw what had happened. Anshu had gone down the slope too fast and the slope had gone around a wide bend. At the bottom it had opened out into what looked like a very large, very muddy and unexpectedly deep pool into which she had splashed and come to a halt. She was now sitting elbow deep in slush, her bike lying beside her. Shiv had promptly followed her in but had stayed upright on his bike. Pankaj and Nasreen had managed to stop just at the edge of the pool and were laughing fit to bust, even as Lavina and I untangled ourselves from one another. The dogs were already cooling off in the muddy water.

'Oh blast it!' Anshu said, struggling to her feet and looking at herself and spitting grit out of her mouth. 'I just never saw it coming.'

'You went straight in,' Shiv hooted, grinning. 'Like one of those crazy rally bikers.'

'Very funny! But just look at me.' She was pretty much covered with mud from head to toe.

'It's just mud, Anshu,' Pankaj said solemnly. 'Like a mudpack. All animals give themselves mud-baths. It's good for their skins. It has medicinal qualities.'

'I'll give you medicinal qualities in a minute, see how you like it,' Anshu growled, glowering at him. She made a face. 'And yuck, I'm stinking.'

'It has healing powers,' Pankaj went on seriously. 'But you'd better wash your hair properly later. There are probably creepy-crawlies in this mud too.'

Anshu pulled her once pristine maroon X-Raider out of the mud and gazed at it sadly. 'Just look at it!' Shiv helped her pull it out of the pool. Then he extended a hand and began helping her out. She was still knee-dip in the slush which seemed not to want to let go of her. Suddenly Shiv lost his grip and Anshu gave a small scream and fell back into the pool with a gloopy splash. She glared angrily at Shiv who was snorting with laughter.

'You ass, you did that deliberately!'

'Sorry!' Shiv snorted, not sounding at all sorry. He extended a hand again. This time Anshu yanked hard and Shiv went tumbling head over heels into the pool.

'Yikes!' he squawked.

Nasreen flashed a grin and gave poor Pankaj a shove and sent him headlong into it. But she lost her balance and tumbled right after him.

'Oh, just look at them,' Lavina cried, horrified. 'They're like those little piglets in the water channels at India Gate.' She looked at me. 'No, no, don't you dare!' she shrieked but it was too late as I gave her a push. She grabbed my hand and dragged me in with her.

There was no looking back after that! Frankly we had the time of our lives. We slopped the mud down each others' backs and into each others' hair. It was as if Holi had come early. At last we sat in a semi-circle looking at each other and giggling uncontrollably. The Six Pack too had lost no time in jumping in with us. They just loved rolling in the stuff and now like little brown bears were lying in the mud, grinning all over their faces.

'What now?' Shiv asked, looking around and suddenly sobering up. 'Where do we go from here?'

'Well,' said Anshu carefully wiping some mud off her hair, 'we might as well carry on. The mud will dry and drop off I hope.'

'Don't worry, it's therapeutic,' Pankaj said again. 'You'll all look beautiful afterwards.'

We really were in a very thickly foliaged part of the forest and had no option: either we went back, or we waded through the pool to the other side about fifteen feet away and carried on, following what I was now thinking was a 'game trail'.

I took out my compass and carefully wiped it clean. We would be heading north-east, which was fine, actually whichever way we went eventually we would emerge in the city somewhere and could find our way back from there.

So muddy from head to toe, but feeling hugely exhilarated, we continued.

'If someone sees us now, they'll think we're some wild people who have been living in these forests for hundreds of years,' Nasreen said, rolling her eyes. 'They'll send National Geographic after us.'

'You know, the Buddha Jayanti Park should be some distance to the west,' Shiv said as we rattled along, shedding globs of drying mud. The dogs were beginning to look weird too, their fur all spiked up with the stuff. This really seemed to be a rather unfrequented section of the Ridge: there were no riding trails here, which normally crisscrossed the forest. We'd often come across horses being ridden in the Ridge—most belonging to the police or the mounted guards at Rashtrapati Bhavan.

About twenty minutes after we left the pool, we seemed to hit a dead end. Ahead, the path ended at an impenetrable wall of keekar trees, which blocked the way and view ahead. We dismounted and looked for a way through them, just to the left and right of the path. The left was impassable. On the right there seemed to be a deep gully running parallel to the path we had biked along.

'Looks like we'll have to go back after all,' Shiv said, shaking his head ruefully. 'What a bummer!'

'Let's eat first,' Anshu said and the others agreed immediately. It was now getting on to about 10.30 and we were beginning to feel ravenous.

Suddenly Dada plunged into the undergrowth on the right side of the path, headlong into the gully, followed by Badi-Dadi and the others. They'd probably scented a mongoose or black-naped hare or maybe just a bandicoot. I went after them, gingerly lowering myself into the gully and hoping there was no more mud and slime at the bottom. The gully sloped downwards, the earth banks on either side with the keekars overhanging it rising higher making it feel rather like a tunnel or canyon almost. Then it turned sharply right and then left again, getting narrower and steeper. The dogs had given up the chase and were now all around me, their tails wagging, their eyes eager. The gully became a dim tunnel under the keekar trees arching over it. Dada bustled past me, brushing against my legs: these guys were having the time of their lives. To my astonishment, the gully opened out into a small oblong moat-like channel nearly completely hidden by the trees growing along its banks. Stone steps led down into it, and across it there looked to be a small rocky wall surrounding a fortress-like structure. A sprawling banyan tree was all over it, like a dome almost. In the wall there was a dark archway, like a doorway and steps leading up into it from the bottom of the 'moat'. Dada and Badi-Dadi had already gone through it, so carefully I followed. The 'doorway' was quite deep and on both sides, steep narrow steps disappeared into the darkness, probably to the wall running around it. I went in further and gasped: it was dark inside the arch and was like entering one of those Roman amphitheatres because there were steps arranged in circles going down, down, down into the blackness. Narrow beams of light speared right down from the stone roof above, where the banyan roots had prised it open. (This structure would have been invisible from above: no drone or satellite would have spotted it—all they would have seen was the canopy of the banyan tree.)

What do you know! Here in the depths of the Ridge, I had found another ancient tomb or hunting lodge-cum-amphitheatre! It had probably been concealed from prying eyes by the banyan tree towering all over it and had remained hidden for God knows how long, guarded by its fearsome phalanx of keekar trees. Of course, its existence must have been known before the trees on the Ridge had been planted, but then over the years it got hidden gradually, and everyone just forgot about it as it disappeared from sight. Wow oh wow! Then I heard a muffled, exasperated shout.

'Umesh, where the hell are you? Get back here this minute!' That was Anshu bellowing for me.

I turned around and made my way back to the others. They were standing at the edge of the gully down which I had plunged and Shiv was about to climb down into it.

'Don't disappear just like that,' Anshu said exasperatedly as I appeared, red-faced and bursting with excitement. 'You can get lost.'

'Anshu and everybody! You won't believe what I found! Yet another hunting lodge and an amphitheatre!'

A few minutes later we found out that I had been almost completely wrong.

4

I proudly led the way as I showed the others my great discovery. We had quite a time lowering the bicycles into the gully and wheeling them through it, but we managed. Anshu was right beside me, tightly holding my hand in case I disappeared again. The others bumped close behind and the dogs had gone on ahead.

'Look,' I said triumphantly, pointing across the 'moat'. 'That is another hunting lodge.'

We went across the grassy moat that had shallow water at the bottom—probably collected after all the rain we had had—and parked our bikes here. I took a casual look at the odometer of my bike: it now read 241.2 km—not a great distance considering how long it had taken us to get here but then that's safari biking for you. This place was about 1.2 km north-east from Malcha Mahal. I followed the others as they went up the steps leading into the building.

'Watch out for bats,' Shiv warned. Anshu and I paused at the edge of the entrance, peering into the darkness beneath.

'There are steps going down,' Anshu said and I nodded.

'It's like an amphitheatre,' I said, keen to show off my vocabulary. She shook her head.

'No, silly, you can't see what's at the bottom by sitting here. So how could you see the actors?'

'Oh,' I said. As usual she was right.

Anshu looked at the rest of us. 'This isn't only a hunting lodge,' she said, shaking her head. 'I think this is a well too—a step well of some kind. I wonder who built this one.' She looked at the others peering over our shoulders. 'Come on guys, let's go down and check it out. Let's see if there's water at the bottom.'

We moved to make room for the others. I flashed my torch at the steps and walls. The steps were built right around the structure, disappearing down into the darkness. Shiv picked up a pebble and tossed it down.

'Shh!' he cautioned and we strained our ears.

We heard the soft echoing plop as the pebble hit the water a few seconds later.

'There's water at the bottom. Come on now, but be careful guys; it may be slippery.'

The dogs were as usual rushing up and down and around the stairs excitedly. We descended cautiously;

it got darker and darker as we went lower and lower. All too soon we could see the dancing reflections of our flashlights bounce back from the black water below. The steps had got narrower and steeper.

Suddenly I stopped as a thought hit me: would these steps also suddenly just end and plunge us into a pit of darkness like the reverse of what had been described in *Kidnapped*? Were we too being lured to our doom? As we climbed down further, it got cool and musty and damp and the old familiar fug of bats was in the air. We spooked several of them and got spooked in turn too.

Then finally, the water lapped at the steps we had reached: we were at the bottom. The steps went down further under the water like those in a swimming pool. The pool was round and maybe 15 feet across. Anshu bent down and scooped up some water in her palms.

'It's cold,' she said, 'just lovely!'

'Don't drink it,' Shiv warned. 'All those bats and god knows how many birds and other creatures must have pooped in it.'

'Man, is this a find or what?' Nasreen said sitting down. She yanked off her muddy hikers and socks and thrust her feet into the water.

'Bliss!' she grinned. 'Sheer bliss!'

'We should call this Umi's well,' Lavina said, standing next to me. 'After all, he discovered it.' I must have gone red in the face with pleasure. It's good to be recognized especially by someone who you hope will be your girlfriend.

'I wonder if there are fish in this well,' Pankaj said, peering into the water, 'or bioluminescent creatures of the deep with venomous entrails and harpoon stings!'

'Don't be idiotic, Pankaj,' Nasreen said.

The dogs had lapped up the water and were now lying down on the steps, quite contented.

'Wonder how deep it is?' Anshu mused and I looked at her sharply. 'Listen,' she went on suddenly, 'I don't know about you guys but I'm going to have a dip. It'll wash all this mud off.'

Five minutes later we were all in the water. It was pretty chilly, especially at first. We could all swim and loved it. Nasreen was easily our champion swimmer. We whooped it up, but not too loudly because our voices tended to echo disconcertingly making us sound hollow and metallic as if we were at the bottom of a metal barrel. It was really too small to swim properly, but we could tread water and stay afloat.

Shiv, Pankaj and I had stripped off our shirts. The girls waded in wearing all their clothes except their denim jackets. Our eyes had got used to the dimness— it wasn't as pitch dark as it had seemed, and the black water was pleated with streaks and flashes of silver light from above. As we sloshed around, the odd beam of sunlight speared right into the water like a silver laser. Sometimes we bumped into one another with surprised squeals.

'This is just great,' Shiv said, treading water in front of Anshu. 'Next time we come here with our swimming trunks and towels and floats.'

'You bet,' Anshu said, her eyes shining. 'This place will be bliss in summer. Cool and dark!'

'Guys, I'm getting out,' Lavina said after some time. 'I'm getting chilled to the bone.'

I watched as she clambered up the steps, water streaming off her. A stray beam of sunlight suddenly lit her up and the water dripped off her nose and chin like a string of silver pearls. She picked up her backpack and I quickly followed her out and we climbed back up together. The others said they'd follow in a while. Panting slightly, we reached the top. In the doorway, I stopped and turned.

'Look, there are narrow stairs going up from the side here,' I said, pointing at the alcove as she stood next to me. 'Want to see where they go? Probably to the wall and battlements.'

'Sure,' she said, 'let's check it out.'

Those steps were very narrow and very steep and went round and round in a spiral. I held on to the walls on either side. And then we stepped out into the dappled sunlight on the wall or battlements of the hunting lodge. The banyan soared above and around, its leaves rustling in a blustery cool breeze. This was probably where the hunters had waited for their prey. Lavina gently bumped into me from behind.

'Wow,' she said, looking around. On one side and below us was the grassy moat where our bikes glittered in the sun, on the other the round bulk of the monument that guarded the step-well beneath it, engulfed by the banyan. But on the battlement wall, there was a small open grassy patch, perfect, I suddenly thought, for drying out my shirt. I'd rinsed my T-shirt out in the pool to rid it of the mud from our mud-bath and now spread it out to dry on the outer ledge of the battlement wall. Lavina looked at it and then arched her eyebrows and smiled.

'That's a good idea!' She rummaged in her backpack and took out a bright yellow hand towel. 'Okay, Umi do me a favour. I'm going to dry myself off and put on my jacket. Be a pet and stay here, will you? I'll just go inside and change. I'm freezing in this top.'

'Sure sure,' I said, reddening, 'I'll be right here.'

A few moments later she hastened out of the staircase.

'Eek! The place is full of Pankaj's precious spiders!' she squealed, looking horrified. I could hear the others: they were still having a good time. Nasreen's gay laughter floated up and Shiv was whooping and then Pankaj must have said something because they all laughed. But I was happy because I was with Lavina, and just hoped she had guessed she was my girlfriend. I joined her on the wall and then sat down, resting my head against it. Lavina, who was facing me, was now lying down on her tummy like a sunbather and seemed to have dozed off—her hair tumbling all over her face. The jacket was a short one and her midriff was bare.

Not quite knowing what to do, I rummaged in my knapsack, looking for an energy bar. My fingers closed over what seemed to be an envelope and puzzled, I pulled it out. It was the envelope Anshu had given me the previous evening, but what the heck was it doing here? Without thinking—I was still really a little mesmerized by Lavina—I opened it and took out the sheets of flimsy pink tissue paper and unfolded them. Immediately, I realized it was absolutely the wrong thing to do.

'What have you got there?' Lavina murmured sleepily, propping herself up on her elbows, hearing the crackling of the sheets.

'Um…nothing…' I mumbled, going hot and cold all over as I tried to fold over the sheets and stuff them back into the envelope. Lavina propped herself higher.

'What is it? Show me,' she leaned forward like a turtle poking its head out of its shell.

'Jj…just a letter for Salim…I opened it by mistake,' I stammered, knowing I was going red.

'What? Let me see!' She reached forward and gently took the sheets from my hand.

'Stop looking down the top of my jacket, you silly boy, you're too young for all that,' she chided me gently. Then she unfolded the roughly folded, half-crumpled sheets. She sat up and her beautiful brown eyes widened as she scanned the letter.

'Oh-oh!' she exclaimed, glancing at me. 'You're right; maybe you shouldn't have opened this.'

'Why? What's in it? I haven't read it.'

'You don't know? Then, well nothing you would understand. Look, we'd better put this back now.' Her face had gone all pink but she was still scanning the letter swiftly, unable to stop reading. By then it was too late. Suddenly the dogs barked happily. The others were on their way up! And those damn dogs led them straight to us. Anshu emerged on the terrace, stopped in her tracks, her jaw dropping in surprise, still dripping from head to toe.

'Wow!' she said, looking around, and then saw Lavina. 'Luv, what's that?' she asked, reaching out. 'What are you reading? That looks like…Who gave you that?' Poor Lavina went absolutely pink.

'Um…um…' she stuttered and meekly handed it over. The others stood there, also dripping, looking puzzled.

It was my big moment. I stood up nobly and took the bullet.

'Anshu, it was my fault,' I said, 'I just opened it by mistake…And…and I gave it to Lavina to read…'

Lavina glanced at me sharply; Anshu was trying desperately to keep the letter dry—and I could see she was wild. There were angry red spots on her cheeks.

'What is wrong with you?' she snapped at me. 'I can't trust you with anything! Why have you brought this here in the first place? You are supposed to give it to Salim tomorrow, not carry it around and read it aloud in public.' Hah, I thought, of course she was mad because I had opened the letter. Especially, since it was a mushy love letter from her to Salim. She wouldn't want the rest of the gang to know that! But…but she wouldn't trust me with anything again…and there was something else. In what little I had seen of the letter it didn't seem to have been in her handwriting…

'So sorry,' I gulped. 'I…I didn't read it out aloud or at all actually but…'

'Just shut up, will you!' She looked at the letter and began folding it as carefully and neatly as she could. 'And you Lavina, you should have had better sense! How would you like it if someone opened and read your private letters?'

Lavina looked sheepishly at the ground, her cheeks and ears turning pink. Then she glanced at Anshu.

'I know, and I'm sorry!' she said; and then added quietly, 'But I think you ought to read that letter too, Anshu.'

'*What?*' my sister exploded.

All this was too much for Shiv. He neatly plucked the letter out of Anshu's fingers and opened it up again and swiftly danced away from her, grinning.

'*Shiv! Give that back to me this instant!*' Anshu yelled, charging after him. Pankaj and Nasreen looked on bemused from the doorway. Shiv dodged away easily even as Anshu went after him and then managed to hold her at bay while he swiftly scanned the letter, grinning away. But then his grin faded suddenly and he dropped his arm as Anshu reached out for the letter.

'Anshu, Lav's right. I think you better read the letter,' he said, handing it over to her meekly.

'Have you all gone mad?' my sister raged. 'Are you all crazy?'

'Um…just read it and then tell us,' Shiv said, exchanging glances with Lavina who was still looking very ashamed.

'I will do no such thing,' my sister raged on. 'My problem is how do I explain the condition of this letter when it is finally delivered?'

'Anshu, read it please,' Lavina pleaded. 'Khushboo could be in bad trouble!'

'What?' Anshu looked sharply from Lavina to Shiv. She sat down on the steps, slowly opened the letter and began reading it. She read it from start to finish and then looked up, shocked.

'Oh my god,' she whispered. 'What can we do about this? We have to do something!' Gently Nasreen took the letter from her and sat down beside her with Pankaj peering over her shoulder.

Great, I thought, sourly, soon it would only be me who had not actually read the letter—and taken the blame for everything. Typical!

They were all sitting down now in the sun on the moat's wall and looking at each other. Nasreen had finished reading the letter and handed it back to Anshu.

'Well,' I said, 'so what's in the letter?'

Anshu glared at me. 'Nothing you need to know,' she said. But I did know a little more than before: I guessed that the letter must have been from Khushboo to Salim and not from Anshu to him. But why were they all looking so upset?

'I...I think we should tell him,' Lavina said at last, 'just so he won't get all kinds of weird ideas.'

'Hmph!' Anshu snorted. 'I suppose so or he'll be spreading all kinds of stories.'

'I do not spread stories,' I protested hotly.

Lavina smiled at me. 'It's like this, Umi. Khushboo

and Salim like—well love—each other very much. But Khushboo's family doesn't like that. They don't let her meet or talk with him anymore; they've forbidden her from doing that.'

I got it. I glanced at Shiv and Pankaj and we sniggered slightly. Then suddenly I sobered down and looked at Lavina. Pankaj was looking with round eyes at Nasreen and Shiv had flicked a glance at Anshu. The smirks were off their faces too. Lavina went on: 'She can't phone him…'

I nodded. Anshu and I knew that. Vineet had smashed Khushboo's phone in front of us. 'And they've taken away her laptop and have more or less locked her up at home.'

'Oh,' my eyes suddenly widened, 'You mean we're like spies picking up and delivering secret messages?'

'Yes, I guess you can put it like that.'

'Too much!' This was thrilling! 'But why don't Khushboo's parents and Vineet like Salim?' I asked. 'He's a great guy. He coaches us so well and he's becoming a doctor.'

Anshu looked a bit uncomfortable and glanced at Nasreen. 'Well, mainly because Khushboo is Hindu and Salim is Muslim and her family can't stomach that! Also, he's not rich. Though why all that should be an issue, I don't know.' We all looked at Lavina who blushed. Her dad was Maharashtrian (with some

Portuguese blood thrown in) and her mom's parents were from either Kyrgyzstan or Uzbekistan (or maybe one from each) and were Muslim and Christian. That made Lavina all mixed-up, just oh so beautiful, like a mixed-fruit smoothie! We had never really consciously thought about her or her parents in that way until now: they were just jolly, happy people who cooked great food!

'And I'll bet Salim's parents don't want him to go around with her for the same reason,' Nasreen now added with some asperity, shaking her head. 'You know what some parents are like!' Quietly she reached out and took Pankaj's hand. He looked a bit bewildered and then went pink. Then she suddenly smiled at him.

'It's okay. Ma and Pa don't mind you showing me spiders and centipedes!' Pink became scarlet.

'And to think Khushboo and Salim both went to our school and have known each other like forever,' Lavina went on. She shuddered. 'Now that horrible Vineet is threatening to hang them both from the same tree if he catches them talking or meeting. Like he's some Hindi-film hero protecting the family's honour.'

'So what's the problem?' I asked, trying to sound more gung-ho than I really felt. Vineet was a nasty piece of work and I was a little scared of him. 'Anshu and I will continue to keep giving the letters like we have been doing. No one will know.'

'We certainly can't give this letter to Salim,' Anshu said, grimacing. 'Just look at it! It looks like a buffalo's chewed it up as cud.' It was looking rather tattered and the blue ink (Khushboo actually used an ink pen, can you imagine) had smudged where wet fingers had grasped it. 'We'll have to tell Khushboo that you dropped it in the potty or in a puddle or something and that she better write another one.'

'Khushboo is clever. She'll know at once that you've read it,' Nasreen pointed out. 'Maybe it would just be better to tell her the truth.'

'I'll come too, if you want. It was partly my fault; I took it from Umi and read it. He'd wanted to put it away,' Lavina said and I fell head over heels in love with her all over again. She was taking the bullet for me!

'Okay, so now that's decided, let's eat,' Anshu said. 'You guys, go down to the bikes and get the food, please. And don't forget the stove.'

Pankaj, Shiv and I went to the bikes and collected the food and plates and things. We'd brought noodles, namkeen, bread, bhuttas, a tin of sausages and dog biscuits and even a couple of packets of tomato soup.

'Pankaj and Umi, go down to the well and fill up these bottles,' Shiv said, 'We'll need the water to boil up the noodles.'

We fetched the water and were on the way up again, when about halfway up I felt one of the bottles slip from my grasp. I set them all down and picked them up again, casually flashing my torch around the well walls. That's when I saw something. I gasped. Right across on the opposite wall was what looked like a black hole: like the opening of a tunnel. Till now we hadn't noticed it because we had only focused on the bottom of the well. Pankaj had gone on up, but the dogs were still with me. So I walked across to the other side and peered into the black hole.

I had made my second great discovery of the day.

There were steps in the doorway plunging deeply downwards into darkness.

When I went back up to the moat terrace, bursting with this news, the picnic was well under way. The noodles were boiling away, and Shiv, Pankaj and Nasreen were roasting bhuttas on a small fire they had made.

'Guys!' I yelled, 'You won't believe what I found!'

'Now what?' Anshu groaned. 'Not again!'

'There's a tunnel opening on the opposite side of the well about halfway down, with steps leading down into the depths,' I said, 'How about that?'

'What? Okay, okay, we'll check it out. But first let's eat. These noodles are about done.'

We checked out the tunnel entrance after we'd eaten. Very proudly, I led the way. The steps spiralled downwards steeply and we had to be careful, holding on to the narrow walls on either side. I had just gone down the second spiral when Anshu suddenly called out from behind, her voice echoing hollowly.

'Listen guys, I think we'd better start getting back. It's already 2.45 and we've got a long way back to go. You know what will happen if we get late. We'll come back here and explore this properly next Sunday.'

I stopped. Lavina was one step below me and now turned around; I was at eye-level with her. Our noses bumped and then she hugged me hard.

'You are such a sweet boy,' she whispered huskily. Then she giggled. 'Now let's go back!' I let her squeeze past me and followed, hoping my face was not totally crimson.

As we gathered our bikes, Anshu looked around solemnly.

'Okay guys, we keep this discovery totally secret, right? We seem to have found a monument that's been forgotten for god knows how many hundred years. If word gets out you know what will happen. You saw what happened at Malcha Mahal this morning. Hordes of people will turn up to swim in their underwear. Ugh! Also, we have to explore that tunnel or whatever it is.' She shrugged. 'It might lead to some royal tomb or ancient buried treasure for all we know. So we keep this to ourselves, okay?'

We all nodded.

'Now let's go back!'

We'd barely started off when the dogs stopped, plunged off the narrow path, southwards through the keekars.

'Hey you guys where the hell do you think you're going?' Anshu yelled, as we skidded to a halt in a line behind her. 'Come back!'

We heard them crashing through the undergrowth and then barking. Then Dada came back poking his head through the trees, grinning all over his face, his tongue hanging out. He barked again and turned and disappeared.

'He...I think he wants us to follow him,' Shiv said, perplexed. 'What the heck is he playing at? Dada, come back here at once. Stop fooling around!'

Again, Dada, this time accompanied by Badi-Dadi, Loafer, Bomber and Badmash, poked his head out and barked impatiently at us.

'I think they've found something,' Nasreen said, 'maybe we should check?'

'It could be someone who's lost and injured,' Pankaj said solemnly, 'someone who's dying and needs help.'

Anshu glared at him.

'Anshu, maybe we should check. If it's a dead rabbit or monkey we'll give the dogs hell,' Nasreen said again.

'I'll go!' I said gamely putting my bike up on its stand. I was feeling quite the pioneering hero this morning: I had made two stupendous discoveries and my girlfriend had hugged me in the dark! Also, I was smaller than the others and could crawl through the thorny stuff more easily.

'Don't go far,' Anshu warned. 'Stay with the dogs.'

The dogs were thrilled that at last someone seemed to be listening to them. They plunged back in full tilt. 'Wait on, not so fast!' I yelled.

At first it was quite tough going through the spiky, prickly thorny stuff. But suddenly I realized that I was on another little 'game trail', hardly discernible but certainly a trail. The dogs, all milling just ahead, kept stopping and waiting for me. No doubt about it, they were on to something. And lo and behold: after a few minutes, this narrow game trail met a much wider trail—one that I could see had been used for horse-riding. It too headed south-east. The dogs just sat down on this trail and looked expectantly at me.

'Okay, so you guys know a shortcut?' I asked. 'Let's call the others.' I went back to where the others were, now getting impatient and a little anxious. 'I think the dogs may have found a shortcut home!'

Well, that's what it turned out to be. We had quite a time bulldozing our bikes through the faint game trail ('We'll bring machetes next time,' Anshu vowed, her face red as she tugged her bike through a thorny bit) but, pricked and scratched and slashed, we finally managed.

From there we cycled fairly easily and swiftly along the horse-riding trail. As long as we headed roughly south-east we were fine and that's the direction this trail went. About twenty minutes later it opened up on the busy main road right opposite which we lived.

'Wow,' Shiv said, glancing at his watch. 'Do you know, it's taken us just forty minutes to get here from the step-well? And we'll be home in five! This morning it took us nearly two hours.'

Tired, dishevelled, scratchy and prickly we were home as we had promised by 4.30, so our parents had almost nothing to complain about. But Ma took one look at Anshu and me, and her eyes widened in horror.

'What on earth have you been doing?' she exclaimed. 'Just look at you! Have you been playing in water? Or with cacti?'

'Yes, sort of, Ma,' Anshu admitted, sounding sheepish. 'You know they water the lawns at Teen Murti and have those sprinklers. We felt hot after cycling so cooled off under them. But we had a really great time!'

'Well you better go and bathe now. They must use sewage water to water the grass there. You'll get some rash!'

⚘

We'd just finished having tea after our baths when Anshu looked at me all flinty. 'We're taking the letter back to Khushboo this evening,' she said, 'she can then write another and you can give it to Salim tomorrow as was the plan.'

I would have much preferred indefinitely postponing the meeting with Khushboo but looked like that was not part of Anshu's plans. 'Okay,' I said reluctantly, 'but Lavina said she wanted to come along too.'

'So call her,' Anshu told me.

I suddenly realized this was something we just *had* to do. Poor Khushboo had been forbidden from meeting or talking to Salim, who she obviously loved and who loved her back. How would I or Lavina like it if we had been forbidden from talking to, or meeting each other?

5

We stood outside Khushboo's house in the small dim lobby and rang the doorbell. All of us were neat and tidy now. Lavina was all fresh and pink. She must have really scrubbed herself. Anshu in jeans and a T-shirt had her blue backpack in which she had kept the tattered letter.

'Give me the letter,' I suddenly said. 'I'll hide it inside my shirt. What if they search your bag?'

She glared at me. 'Don't be silly,' she snapped a little nervously.

The door opened and there was Vineet, looking as if he had just awoken and not shaved for many days, nor brushed his teeth for about two months. He was in a crumpled banian and baggy shorts and had very hairy legs and ugly hairy armpits.

'Who are you and what do you want?' he asked belligerently, scratching his stomach. He peered at us and then seemed to recognize us.

'You've come for tuition?' he asked as we nodded.

'Come in,' he stood aside to let us in. 'Khushboo never said she had tuition today!' We stood around the dining table, nodding stupidly as he went in to call her. We heard a door being unlocked and then opened.

'Khushboo, your students are here: you never said you had tuition today!' He sounded irritated. Then Khusboo Didi entered, looking surprised. She was in a maroon churidar-kurta and there were dark smudges below her eyes and a bruise on her cheek.

'Hello, Anshu dear,' her eyebrows rose inquiringly.

'You can take your class in your room,' Vineet snarled. 'I want to watch the match on TV here.'

Whew! That was a relief. And Khushboo was really smart. She had caught our vibes straight off. She nodded and smiled.

'Come along this way,' she said. Her room was painted light green and one wall was stacked with books. There were more books on her writing desk, but there was no desktop or laptop. The bed had a dark green and yellow bedcover and paintings of wild-flowers on the wall.

'Anshu, what is it?' she asked, quietly shutting the door behind us. Anshu went red.

'Khushboo Didi, I'm sorry but there was an…um… accident,' she said, unzipping her backpack.

It was time for me to be noble for the second time today and take another bullet.

'Didi, by mistake I opened the letter when we went for a picnic to the Ridge this morning,' I gabbled, 'I had put it in my backpack instead of cricket bag...'

'Actually it was my fault: I took it from him and read it first,' Lavina said quickly.

'What? I don't understand...' Khushboo said, frowning. Then Anshu took out the bedraggled letter and handed it over.

'You better write this again. This time I'll make sure that he gives it to Salim Bhai properly.'

'Oh...oh,' Khushboo said quietly, suddenly sitting down on the bed and taking the letter from Anshu. 'I...I guessed this would happen at some point... but...' She looked at us.

'Don't worry, Didi, your secret is safe with us,' I solemnly said, nodding. 'You and Salim Bhai can keep writing letters and we'll deliver them, no problem.'

She glanced at the letter, her cheeks turning pink. To my horror I saw there were tears in her lovely brown eyes. Anshu and Lavina sat beside her.

'Don't cry, Didi,' Anshu said, 'We're all on your side.'

'We like Salim Bhai, too,' I added virtuously. 'He's a very good coach.'

She looked at us one by one and smiled through her tears.

'Thank you,' she said softly, 'you all are very sweet kids.' She looked at the letter in her hand and took a deep breath. 'Okay, I'll write him another letter.' Then she looked suddenly doubtful. 'Are you sure it's all right? If Vineet finds out…he can be very unpleasant.'

'It'll be fine, no one will suspect us,' Anshu shrugged. 'We're just kids, after all, what do we know?'

Lavina suddenly looked towards the door, an expression of panic on her face. Khushboo too looked up. (I was too busy staring at Lavina).

'Anshu,' Lavina hissed warningly.

Anshu did not hesitate for a second. She just snatched the letter out of Khushboo's hands and stuffed it into her backpack just as the door burst open and Vineet barged in. Anshu's hands were still in her backpack and now, as we watched with horror, she took them out again…holding her school workbook. My sister was a born spy!

'Didi,' she said brightly, and then stopped as Vineet stepped into the room and looked around suspiciously.

'I couldn't quite solve the last two Algebra problems you set me,' she went on and once again I was amazed at her attention to detail. The notebook she was holding in her hands indeed was her Algebra notebook! Lavina looked gobsmacked too.

'Khushboo, where do you people keep the sugar and tea?' Vineet demanded. 'I can't find them. Also, there are no soda bottles in the fridge. You know Biker will be coming over later, and he has soda with his drinks.'

'I'll just make you some tea, Bhaiyya. And then after the class I'll buy the sodas,' Khushboo said, getting up.

Vineet compressed his lips. 'Take the children with you and let them drop you back here too,' he said. 'You know you are not allowed to go about alone and I don't want to miss the match.' He smiled at us. 'Didi gets dizzy from time to time and can fall, so the doctor has said she should not be allowed to go out all by herself.'

'All right, Bhaiyya,' we said together, 'we'll take her and bring her back.' Anshu added an angelic smile.

He left the room with Khushboo and we looked at each other.

'Anshu, you're something else,' Lavina said admiringly.

'This is so cool,' I whooped, 'like a spy thriller.'

Anshu looked at Lavina. 'This is about true love,' she declared solemnly, her eyes bright. 'Nothing must come in the way of true love.'

I looked at Lavina, my face going hot again. I couldn't agree more.

My sister sighed dramatically. 'And Khushboo must never be forced to marry that Biker creep if she doesn't want to,' she declaimed, her eyes flashing. 'Biker!' she shuddered, 'what a name!'

Suddenly the door opened again and Vineet entered alone. He nodded at us. 'Khushboo is making tea,' he announced. He looked at us one by one and nodded.

'I'm sorry about what happened the other day,' he said surprisingly. 'I lost my temper and you must think I'm some sort of rakshas brother. But it's for her own good. She makes friends with all kinds of undesirable people.' Then he reached into his pocket. He took out a 500-rupee note and held it out to me.

'Come here you and listen to me,' he said, obviously thinking I was the boss here. He patted my head as though I were one of the Six Pack. 'When you go with Khushboo to the shop make sure she doesn't talk to anyone. If she says she wants to phone someone get the number or try and hear what she says to that person. Then come and tell me. Some bad people have gotten after her—and you know how beautiful she is. If anyone follows her, tell me. Okay?'

Astounded, we nodded dumbly. He was the father of all Jekyll and Hydes!

'Here,' he said handing me the money. 'This is for you all. There will be more.'

I didn't know whether to take the money or not so looked at Anshu. She nodded, so I took it.

'Thanks, we'll let you know. How do we contact you? Should we come here?'

'This is my number,' he said, scribbling it down and handing it over. 'If there is anything important to report, let me know immediately.'

'Okay, sir!'

'What is your name?' he asked me suddenly.

'Dada,' I blurted, 'they call me Dada.'

Anshu and Lavina looked at me with round eyes. Then they nodded.

'Good, okay Dada you know what to do.' He got up and left the room, leaving us staring at each other. Quickly I pocketed the money.

'The slimeball!' Anshu said softly, 'Imagine, he wants us to spy on his own sister.'

'We should tell Khushboo at once,' Lavina said. Suddenly I grinned. Hah! That stupid Vineet thought he was so damned smart but he had just recruited double agents to do his dirty work.

'Of course, we will tell her,' Anshu said. She looked at me. 'And we give her the money Vineet gave us—so take it out of your pocket, mister.'

'Dada!' Lavina snorted suddenly. 'Why did you say your name was Dada?'

'I couldn't give him my real name! Spies never do. They always have aliases.'

A few minutes later Khushboo was back. She shut the door and looked at us, smiling.

'You monkeys are something else,' she said, going to

her desk. She pulled out a writing pad and unscrewed a dark-blue fountain pen: a Cross, I think. As she wrote, her face too turned pink and then solemn. We exchanged glances and waited quietly. At last she finished and sealed the letter in another envelope. Then she came up to me.

'Here you are, Umesh,' she said holding me by the shoulders. 'Will you please give this to Salim Bhai?'

I nodded and she kissed my forehead. 'Bless you,' she said quietly. Anshu cleared her throat.

'Err, Didi,' she said, 'Vineet was here just now. He… he wants us to spy on you; to tell him if you speak to or meet or phone anyone when you come with us to the shop. He even gave us five hundred rupees to do that!'

Shock and then anger flashed in Khushboo's eyes.

'And what did you say?'

'We agreed, of course,' Anshu said, fishing out the money and handing it over. 'Only Vineet doesn't know we're working for you.'

Khushboo shook her head. 'I really don't know whether I should have got you kids mixed up in all this,' she said. 'But should we all now go down to the bania's and get some soda? And I think some Magnum ice creams will be in order for you all.' She grinned, and held up the note. 'After all, Vineet Bhaiyya is paying!'

'Do you really get dizzy?' Anshu asked her as we set off. Khushboo shook her head.

'No, of course I don't. They just don't want me to go out alone. I have to go either with Mama or Vineet or Papa. They've tried to keep me at home but find it difficult to make sure someone is home with me all the time. Mama and Papa have work and Vineet likes roaming around with his horrible friends too much! If I say I want to go to the park for a walk, they come along for that too.'

'But now you can come along with us,' Anshu said as another wicked smile lit up her face.

Lavina grinned. 'And we don't mind where you want to go or who you want to meet.'

Khushboo's face had lit up.

'You kids are really something else,' she said again. 'I'm so grateful to you.'

Later that evening after buying the sodas we dropped Khushboo back home. All her cheeriness over the ice creams she had bought for us vanished as she opened the door to step inside.

'That ghastly Biker is coming for dinner and he and Vineet will be drinking all night,' she told us. 'They become loud and obnoxious when they do that and expect me to sit with them and serve them snacks. They say they want to go into business together but never seem to be actually doing anything about it. So they drink and talk loudly and expect me to stand around to serve them all the time. And if I refuse…'

She left that last sentence unfinished. We knew what came after. That bruise on her cheek was enough. Sadly, we still didn't have an idea what we could do to help her about that.

⤜⊙⊙⤛

The next day, I got back from school and went down to the grounds for cricket coaching. Shiv came along with me.

'I have the replacement letter,' I told him sotto voce. Briefly I told him of what had happened. In the ground, Salim, perfectly kitted out in cricketing whites, came up to us.

'Hi boys, come along and begin your warm-up.'

I fished out the envelope. 'Salim Bhai, this is for you,' I whispered tersely looking around the empty park.

'Thank you,' he said quietly, taking it.

As we began our exercises and jogging, he sat down on the grass and read the letter. I kept glancing sideways at him, but couldn't really make out the expression on his face because it was in shadow.

Then again we heard the rasp of bike engines. This time there were four of them: Vineet, Biker and two other unsavoury types. Thankfully they didn't interfere with us, just watched and sniggered among themselves. Salim ignored them.

We were packing up our kit after coaching when he came up to me. To my surprise he had the same envelope in his hand. Oh god, I thought, was he returning her letter? Had he spurned her love? Had he dumped her?

'Please give this to your sister to give it to the person who had given it to her to give to me,' he said, befuddling me for a second. He saw my expression and clarified. 'My reply is in that, I didn't have an envelope, you see!'

'No problem, Salim Bhai,' I plucked the envelope smartly out of his hand. I was getting good at this spy business, too.

Well, that's how it started. And boy did it gather a momentum all of its own! Lavina and Nasreen signed up for tuition with Khushboo the very next day, so that she basically had a tuition class every day. And every single day notes or letters would be exchanged. It was hugely exciting. And what do you know, Vineet had also become friendly with us in a sickly, plastic sort of way. We were constantly in and out of their house and Anshu said that he probably thought that we were, in addition to spying for him, also diverting her attention from Salim, which was a good thing as far as he was concerned. After the first outing to the bania's I had reported to him that nothing suspicious had occurred. So he asked us if we could accompany her to the shops and when she did other chores. Every time he paid us! We had no adverse reports to give him. Which was true: she really did not meet anyone or speak to anyone or phone anyone when she came out with us. She only wrote and received love letters. And bought us ice creams and pizzas with the money Vineet had given us to spy on her! It was a perfect set-up! It was a shame that her horrible family had practically made her a prisoner and a brilliant student like her was studying her Masters in History by correspondence. But my eyes were sharp, and I had seen she had brought in papers for various competitive exams and was probably preparing for those. Khushboo was too smart to stay under her family's thumb for too long!

That awful Biker was often at their house when we went for tuition. I had also begun accompanying Anshu Didi in order to 'improve my English' and figure out what the hell was happening in *Kidnapped*. Once, he even came to the dining room where we were sitting and put his hands on Khushboo's shoulders and squeezed them in front of all of us even though she grimaced and squirmed as though a centipede had crawled over her.

Then my sister decided to take all this jasoosi to another level.

'You know,' she told Lavina and Nasreen one evening after we'd returned from tuition. 'So far they've only exchanged notes and letters. The poor things haven't even been able to meet each other. They must be dying to.'

'So what are you thinking?' Lavina asked. 'We inform Salim when she will be going to the supermarket or to Mother Dairy next so they can secretly meet there?'

'Nah, don't be nuts! We'll think of something…'

I had a brainwave. 'Anshu, you have History tuition with Khushboo, don't you?'

'Yes, so?'

'So why don't you ask her to take you—and all of us—to historical monuments in Delhi? Salim can meet her there!'

Anshu looked at me and suddenly hugged me. 'That's brilliant! Sometimes you really are a very clever fellow,' she said, kissing my cheek and Lavina gave me a quick hug too.

'Imagine, they could meet and hold hands at Lodi Gardens and Sundar Nursery and Humayun's Tomb and…'

We would have to set up the dates and timings perfectly to make this work. We couldn't wait to tell them of our new idea.

At the next class we did.

'Tomorrow afternoon instead of us coming here for tuition could we all go to Lodi Gardens instead? You could teach us about the monuments there and all,' Anshu asked her innocently. Then she leaned forward and lowered her voice. 'Umesh will tell Salim Bhai you'll be there, so…'

Khushboo cocked her head (like Lady Bouncer), and her eyebrows shot up.

'Yes,' I said, 'Salim Bhai could easily give us coaching class there.'

'Or if you like we could go to the Nehru Memorial Museum and Library and you could tell us about our great leaders and Independence fighters and all that… It's much closer too…'

Khushboo started smiling and I understood why Salim loved her so much. 'Yes,' she said softly, reaching out and pinching our cheeks, 'that is a very good idea indeed.' She swallowed. 'Let me know where you would like to go, you lovely wicked, wicked children!'

'We'll ask Salim Bhai and get back to you tomorrow morning with all the details,' I said.

Salim tried not to appear embarrassed when Shiv and I told him that we were trying to set up a rendezvous for him with Khushboo.

'It was Anshu's idea,' I told him. 'She said you must be dying to meet and talk to each other. So can you make it tomorrow afternoon? At 3.30?'

He got over his embarrassment and suddenly looked excited. 'Okay,' he said. 'Tomorrow afternoon at Lodi Gardens. I'll be at Gate Number 3 near the Tower. Nehru Memorial is too close for comfort. And thanks, guys!'

And so the first secret meeting was set up. Vineet was relieved that he would not have to tag along when Khushboo was getting out of the house. Perhaps he thought she had gotten over Salim. She was more cheerful and seemed completely involved in her tuitions with us. He had no objection to her taking us to Lodi Gardens for a history class: besides he knew that we would report any hanky-panky back to him the moment it happened, ha-ha!

We picked up Khushboo the following afternoon and set off for Lodi Gardens by auto and the Metro. We were very excited. I kept a sharp eye out for anything suspicious—Vineet following us for example, but the coast seemed clear. We were at Gate No. 3 of Lodi Gardens at 3.25 p.m. To our delight, Salim was already there, pacing up and down impatiently and looking at his watch.

'He's there,' I said tersely.

'Okay, guys, we'd better give them some privacy,' Anshu said, as Khushboo and Salim approached each other slowly, nervously looking around, as if they had just come out of jail after many years.

'Sikander Lodi's tomb is a good place to go if you want some privacy,' my sister cheekily advised them.

'There are usually not too many people there. We'll meet back here in an hour.'

Khushboo blushed as she looked at us. Salim was looking acutely embarrassed as he put his arm around her waist. Then they started walking off arm-in-arm in a manner that would have brought frowns on the brows of all the auntijies and unclejies.

I was suddenly uneasy about the situation. There were so many people in the park—picnickers, families, kids, joggers, walkers and even school parties. It was quite likely that Salim or Khushboo could bump into someone they knew. And then…

'You know, we'd better think of less crowded places for these secret meetings,' I said. 'Someone is sure to see them and then may and go and tell Vineet.'

Anshu nodded. 'Yes, I thought of that too. Our next field trip will be to Safdarjung's Tomb.'

'We could go to Tughlakabad Fort too,' Pankaj suggested. 'It only has monkeys.'

'That's too deserted, which means we'll have to take the Six Pack with us. How are we going to do that?' Shiv asked.

'We could take them to Malcha Mahal,' I said suddenly. 'That's close by and usually there isn't anyone around and we can take the dogs too!'

I glanced at Lavina, looking so beautiful as usual. She was in a short pink skirt that swirled when she walked and a white and light pink top. Hopefully something had begun between her and me too at Malcha Mahal and the secret hunting lodge we had discovered afterwards.

'Are we going to the secret hunting lodge tomorrow?' I asked Anshu. 'We still have to explore that second tunnel-like entrance and see where it leads.'

'I guess we could in the morning.'

We'd brought Frisbees along, thinking we would play with them, but this fear about someone spotting Khushboo and Salim together began bugging me no end. I took this spying business very seriously.

'Anshu, I think we should follow them and form a security cordon so we can warn them if any known person approaches,' I said.

They all looked shocked. 'You want us to play Peeping Tom?' Anshu said, appalled, and yanking my ear. 'You should be ashamed!' Shiv and Pankaj didn't look quite as shocked.

'No,' I shook my head vigorously. 'Suppose they get rumbled? Suppose someone who knows them sees them and informs Vineet?'

'And how will we recognize anyone who may know them?' Nasreen asked. 'We don't know everyone they know.'

'Well, anyone who approaches too close to them maybe then.'

'Humph!'

But Anshu's eyes had narrowed and I knew she was thinking like I was. It would be disastrous if this whole thing unravelled just because some auntieji or uncleji who lived in our colony and who was walking here too spotted them.

'Okay,' Anshu said at last. 'I think we should at least keep a watch for anyone from our colony or school, or anyone we know who might recognize them. We have to give them cover.' We wandered off towards the walled-in tomb, which looked like a miniature fortress. There was just one entry gate—a good thing, where two fellows with their girlfriends were posing for selfies. Lavina, Nasreen and Anshu decided to enter the walled-in garden.

'You guys stay here and keep your eyes peeled. We'll check out inside to see if they are all right and come back.' They slipped in. We stood casually around the gate, looking at the water in the channel and the fountain playing. Beyond it was the old hunched stone bridge.

'I'm going around the wall,' I told the other two. 'You guys keep watch here.' I walked nonchalantly along the wall, momentarily distracted by a pair of crazy squirrels chasing each other as I turned the corner and then:

'Hello Umesh, how nice to see you bachche! Good afternoon! Are you here with your sister?'

Startled, I looked up. I'd nearly bumped straight into Suchitra ma'am, our English and History teacher at school! For some reason, I was a great favourite of hers. She was a short squat lady, with a lot of make-up on her face and was wearing a flowery red and yellow salwar-kameez. She had stringy grey hair in an untidy bun and a wrinkled but kind face. She was a nice person, patient and quite lenient while marking and thought that everyone should only learn History and English. She had taught at our school for donkeys' years.

'Hel…hello…good afternoon, ma'am!' I mumbled. 'Yes, Anshu is somewhere here. We've come here with our friends.'

'I hope you've read up a little about these beautiful monuments,' she said, waving a hand at the monument. 'You know, this is the tomb of Sikander Lodi. By the way, where is your sister? She said she'd been taking coaching classes in History and English from our very own Khushboo.' She had taught Khushboo too, who had also graduated from our school. 'She really couldn't have a better tutor. That girl was just brilliant. She got 98.5 per cent marks in History in her Boards!' Suchitra ma'am was prattling on and on.

'My sister is exploring inside,' I said, nodding virtuously. 'She's very interested.'

'Good, let's join her then. She shouldn't have left you to wander about on your own though.'

'It's okay, my friends are here, too,' I repeated.

Grim-faced, I walked back towards the entrance with her. Pankaj and Shiv, who were playing some game in the dust, looked up. Pankaj looked shocked, Shiv as though he were trying not to laugh. But they both stood up quickly and dusted down their hands.

'Good afternoon, ma'am,' they chorused.

'Ma'am, you wait here. I'll just fetch Anshu,' I gabbled. I yanked Shiv by the collar and hissed in his ear:

'Keep her occupied while I fetch the others.' Then I fled into the big square garden. It had several large trees in which parakeets were noisily squabbling. I went clockwise around the monument and rounded a corner and then backed away quickly my face going red.

Khushboo and Salim were tightly embracing and smooching behind (but not quite hidden by) a big neem tree. I felt a hand grip my shoulder and another quickly cover my mouth.

'You are a nasty little Peeping Tom after all,' Anshu hissed in my ear, putting me in a chokehold. 'How disgusting!'

I freed myself. 'Anshu, Suchitra ma'am from school is just outside. She wants to come in and show us around!'

'What?'

'Yes! Any second she'll come in and…'

Anshu looked around, not knowing what to do. Lavina too looked stunned as I sidled to her side.

It was Nasreen who finally saved the day. She put two fingers into her mouth and whistled; she could stop a train with that whistle I thought, wincing. Immediately, Khushboo and Salim separated and looked towards her. Nasreen gestured with both hands that they stay apart and then beckoned them over. Anshu and Lavina ran up to Khushboo, who was settling her dupatta and smoothing her hair, her cheeks pink and flushed. She looked very happy. Salim looked befuddled and embarrassed: but then they glanced at each other and their eyes kind of lit up again. Anshu and Lavina said something to Khushboo who murmured in turn to Salim. He nodded and they kissed again before he moved away, and disappeared behind the monument. Then the four of us, the three girls and I, along with Khushboo made our way to the entrance, as she began lecturing to us about the tomb. We met Suchitra ma'am and the other two guys just coming through. Those fellows were looking pretty panicky because they had not been able to hold back ma'am.

'Suchi ma'am!' Khushboo squealed and rushed into our teacher's arms. 'How lovely to see you!'

'I believe you've taken Anshu under your wing,' Suchitra ma'am said, hugging her back. 'She couldn't get a better tutor. She's shown a remarkable improvement in her tests.'

'And all of us too,' Nasreen and Lavina chimed in. 'She's giving all of us tuition. We're all going to do brilliantly now.'

Luckily Suchitra ma'am left us after a while to continue with her walk. We quickly checked back at the tomb of Sikander Lodi but Salim had gone. That didn't bother Anshu very much though.

'You know, tomorrow afternoon we could go to Malcha Mahal for a field-trip,' she said, grinning mischievously as we settled down in the Metro on the way back. 'Very few people go there and we could take the Six Pack along too, as guards.'

Khushboo smiled. 'You'll have to check with Salim if it is convenient,' she said. 'What time do you have in mind?'

'Afternoon. Same as today. Sure, we'll confirm with him. Pankaj will deliver the message.'

Khushboo was beaming. 'And thank you very much for what you did for us today.'

Since we were 'spying' for Vineet too, we had to report to him about the Lodi Gardens trip: after all this had been the first major outing that Khushboo had been allowed on in a long time. And he was paying us too!

'We're dropping you home,' Anshu told Khushboo, grinning. 'We have to report to Vineet about you now.'

For a moment Khushboo looked angry, then she smiled.

'So what are you going to tell him?'

'The truth: that we met Suchitra ma'am who was very glad that you are giving us tuition…'

Khushboo looked at Anshu in silence for a moment and then enclosed her in a tight hug, and then all of us, turn by turn. 'Thank you, kids,' she said, 'but please be careful. Vineet is very unpredictable and can hurt you.'

Sure enough, Vineet escorted us home once we had dropped Khushboo back.

'It's getting dark,' he said, winking hideously as he met us at the front door. 'I'll walk you all home.' He was behaving as though we were in this great secret conspiracy together.

We'd barely reached the ground floor, when he suddenly changed his spots and brusquely asked, 'Well, did she meet anyone?'

We nodded. 'Yes, we met our—and her—old History teacher, Suchitra Dalal ma'am,' Lavina said.

'Oh,' he said, losing interest. '*Theek hai*, if she meets anyone else, inform me immediately.'

'We're going on a field trip tomorrow too,' Anshu said, and I wondered whether she ought to have said that. Malcha Mahal was very close by and the fellow could easily check it out for himself if he knew we were going there. Lavina chimed in: 'We haven't yet decided exactly where to go: the Red Fort or Qutub or Humayun's Tomb…'

Wow, I thought, and Anshu had once said that Lavina didn't have brains? If this wasn't quick thinking, what was?

I for one was looking forward to our expedition to the secret hunting lodge tomorrow.

6

We were at the hunting lodge cum step-well by 9.30 the next morning. The shortcut the dogs had shown us was really a boon, though we did get scratched and pricked a bit more on this route. But from home it hardly took us thirty-five minutes if we didn't dilly-dally on the way. This time we had carried flashlights—Shiv had his new beautiful black Maglite, which he was dying to show off. The place was deserted and quiet; only the huge banyan rustled and creaked in the cool breeze. Suddenly there was a ruckus from the undergrowth, and a chorus of harsh 'kay-kay-kay' calls startled us. Mousy grey-brown birds with hard pale-yellow eyes were rummaging about the leaves tossing them this way and that.

'They're large grey babblers,' Pankaj informed us. 'They look angry but they love cuddling up together.' I quickly sidled up to Lavina and tried to catch her eye.

'Okay guys, let's see where this goes,' Anshu said as

we stood and looked at the black hole in the wall. She frowned. 'I think we ought to bring our bikes inside and park them along the steps before we go down,' she said. 'They'll be safer there. Who knows where this goes and how long we'll be gone.'

It was a good idea though as usual my sister was trying to psyche us.

'And so we descend into the bowels of hell,' Shiv intoned sepulchrally, flashing his torch into the darkness. He led the way down, followed by Anshu and then Pankaj and Nasreen. Lavina and I brought up the rear. Again, I really thought I ought to have been leading because it had been my discovery but it was okay because suddenly Lavina's soft hand reached out and took mine. We were secretly holding hands! The dogs as usual kept going back and forth, brushing past us to get ahead and then letting us pass them.

The stairs descended for quite some time and then widened into a small space where we all gathered. Ahead there seemed to be the beginning of the tunnel proper.

'Wow!' Shiv breathed, flashing his powerful torch into the mouth of the tunnel. I flashed my light all around. The roof was rounded and made of rocks, and a few straggly roots had tried to push themselves through the joins. But it was a man-made tunnel all right.

'Does anyone have a candle? Before we go any

further we need to check if the air is all right. We could suffocate or die if there's poisonous gas.'

'It seems okay, Anshu,' Lavina said. She was still holding my hand.

'Okay,' Anshu said a bit doubtfully, 'But if any of you feel uneasy, like you can't breathe properly, please shout. This might just be connected to sewer lines and they produce all kinds of gases.'

'Methane and hydrogen sulphide,' Pankaj said, 'but they both stink. But there's also carbon dioxide. That's heavier than air so it will affect the dogs first, so we should watch them. And carbon monoxide—that's deadly!'

Cautiously, we moved on ahead. At places the tunnel walls narrowed, and we had to squeeze through single file but mostly we could walk two abreast. I glanced sideways at Lavina. We were pretty close together, my shoulder bumping against her bare arm frequently. Touching her even just like this made me feel so happy. The rocky roof above seemed solid, and underfoot at places it was wet and slippery with moss and slime. It was musty but not suffocating or anything like that.

'Umesh, you have a compass?' Shiv asked. 'In what direction are we heading?'

'Due east,' I said, flashing my torch at my compass.

'I wonder how long this tunnel is,' Pankaj said.

'And where it leads to,' Anshu added. 'Everyone's breathing okay? No one's feeling short of breath or anything?'

'All good, Anshu!' we chorused.

We walked on, falling silent as we wondered where the heck we were heading.

'How far have we gone?' Shiv asked after a bit. I looked at my Fitbit, which I had set at the start.

'Just about 740 metres,' I said. It had felt much longer.

A little later Shiv shouted back, 'Hey guys there are steps going up ahead. I think we're reaching the end.'

'We can't be,' Pankaj argued, 'there's no light at the end of the tunnel as yet!'

'Very funny!'

We stopped at the bottom of the steps and looked up. It was a comparatively shallow flight going straight up to a wall or something. I glanced at my Fitbit again; we'd now come 750 metres.

'Just imagine, we might just pop up in the middle of Connaught Place,' Anshu said.

'Or yet another secret hunting lodge,' Nasreen added.

'Or in the Lok Sabha where they are always fighting. What a scare we'll give them, serves them right for making hulla all the time instead of working,' Lavina giggled. And Anshu had said she didn't have brains! Man, that was brilliant. Daringly I squeezed Lavina's hand to show I approved.

One by one the dogs went up, followed by Shiv and Anshu and then the rest of us. There was a small landing at the top. It was too small to accommodate all of us, so we sort of queued up on the stairs.

'Seems to be a door here,' Shiv said, flashing his torch at the 'wall' and tapping it. 'Yup, there's a handle here too!'

'Oh I bet it's locked,' Pankaj said. 'But try to open it anyway.'

We waited with bated breath as Shiv pressed down on the heavy-looking brass handle. It creaked and squealed but it went down. Then he pushed against the door. Nothing happened.

'Give it a bit of shoulder,' Anshu said impatiently. Shiv did. There was a shower of dust which turned our light beams into sabres of white light and poor Shiv nearly fell forward and then backed away coughing. We took out our handkerchiefs and covered our mouths and noses and momentarily closed our eyes. The door creaked and wheezed and squealed in protest, but it had suddenly swung open. Shiv poked his head holding his Maglite.

'There's a small room here, like a little hallway,' he reported, 'there seems to be another door straight ahead.' We crowded into the small room as Shiv jiggled the handle of the second door.

'Shoulder again, Shiv,' Anshu ordered.

The second door opened with a jerk, and another cloud of dust. 'There's a short narrow passage leading into a room,' Shiv said, stepping into the corridor. 'It looks like quite a large room out here,' he went on as we all followed. The dogs had rushed in past us already and gone in.

'Look, it's even furnished,' Anshu said, 'though everything's been covered.' There were huge lumpy masses covered in yellowing sheets, looking quite ghostly. What appeared to be chairs, tables, dressers, and against the left wall there stood what appeared to be a bed covered with lumpy-looking things. Everything was covered in dust.

'My god, Anshu, where do you think we've come?' Lavina whispered. 'It's like an old abandoned room!'

'Must be haunted,' Pankaj said decisively, moving ahead cautiously. 'It has to be!'

'Look,' I said, 'there's a switchboard there on the wall.'

'Look at those switches, they're ancient!'

'Better not touch them,' Anshu warned but Shiv had already reached up. The switches were old fashioned up-and-down spring-loaded ones, made of black plastic. He flipped one down. Nothing happened. Then he flipped down another one. A bulb, probably 40 watts, glimmered weakly from a bracket light festooned with cobwebs on the wall. Now we could see the room better. It had no windows. There was the huge bed against the left wall with cushions and pillows probably dumped on it and what seemed like a sofa and three shrouded chairs around a low table at the far end. Large wardrobes loomed up like sentinels along the wall. Two musty drapes lined the wall on the right-hand side; probably there were doors behind them.

'Wow,' Anshu whispered. 'Ghost furniture! Let's get these covers off but carefully. They must be full of dust or moths.'

Carefully we stripped the ancient yellowing sheets off the furniture as dust clouds arose, making us cough. Tentatively I peeked behind one of the drapes on the wall: yes, there was a door there, too. Again, with a bit of shoving it gave, loosening another cloud of dust and revealing another small room. My flashlight picked out a granite table-top running along the far wall on which was placed a rusty two-burner stove. A small rust-speckled white fridge stood against another wall. This was a small kitchen.

'Guys, look at this! An old fridge!'

Lavina came up alongside. 'Hey just look at all these cupboards too. They are filled with jars and china and utensils and stuff.'

'What is this place?' Anshu whispered.

'Hey, Umesh, anything in the fridge? But watch it! There may be a chopped-up body or skeleton waiting to jump out!'

I yanked it open and stepped back retching. Ugh! It stank! But it was empty.

Lavina was checking out the cupboards with the china and utensils.

'My god,' she said, 'these cups and saucers and bowls are really fancy. They look like bone china.' She took out a cup and wiped it with her T-shirt. 'It's all gilded! Look at it, it's beautiful.' It was: a small coffee cup in maroon and gold. Carefully Lavina extracted a plate from the top of a pile. 'This is like cutlery used by royalty. It's all gold and purple and has a coat of arms.'

'Let's check the cupboards,' Nasreen said. 'There may be gold or jewels or stashes of cash!'

We yanked open one of the tall cupboards in the room and got another shock. Stacked from top to bottom were ancient rusting cans of food.

'Just look at these,' Anshu said, taking a couple of tins out as we flashed our torches at the supermarket-like pile. She began reading the labels: '"Heinz Beanz", "Hunter's Steak and Kidney Pudding" what on earth is that? "Fancy Red Salmon", "Pure Dried Powdered Eggs", "Pik Nik Peanut Butter", "Bird's Custard Powder", "Fancy Red Salmon",' she reeled off. 'And there are tins of fruit juice and soups and bottles of lemonade and soda and ginger ale.'

'This is like some ancient bania's dukaan,' Nasreen snorted. 'But who do you think would eat tinned stuff in those fancy plates?'

'Do you think this stuff is still good to eat?' Pankaj asked hopefully. Anshu gave him a withering look.

'They've been locked in this cupboard for god knows how long, the tins are rusty and pitted and some are swollen. They'll probably go off like bombs if we open them.'

'Bombs!' I said suddenly, smacking my forehead, 'Of course! That's what this room is.'

'What?'

'An underground bomb shelter! Look, all this stuff goes back to the 1940s when the World War was on. Some chicken-hearted but very rich Brits must have built this shelter under their house fearing the Japs might bomb Delhi as they had bombed Kolkata. They even dug an escape tunnel all the way to the Ridge. But then the War got over and they and everyone else must have just forgotten about the place.'

They stared at me amazed. (I told you I was not the gang's analytical whiz for nothing.)

'Let's check out the other cupboard.' We yanked it open, sneezing as the dust blew into our faces.

It was stacked with gas masks and khaki tin helmets. And a big green tin with a red cross on it marked 'First Aid'.

'Hey guys, look at this,' I said, crouching down and flashing my torch at the bottom shelf. 'This looks like an old car battery and a transmitter and receiver set.'

'Spies!' said Pankaj. 'It must have been a secret spy hideout!'

'Or else,' Shiv went on frowning, 'the Brits who lived here were very important people who needed to communicate in case they were trapped here or bombed. Man, oh man, Anshu, this is even better than your Malcha Mahal Begum story!'

Nasreen had wandered off to the far side of the room, parting the second set of drapes and pushing open the door behind that. 'There's a bathroom here,' she announced. 'Let me check if the taps work.' We heard several explosive farty noises and then a gurgle.

'Eureka!' Nasreen yelled, 'there's rusty water still spitting out, can you imagine!'

'You know,' Shiv said suddenly. 'This might just be the secret hideout of some serial criminal who has either died or been caught.'

'Must have been a very rich fellow to have built this room and stashed away all of this,' Nasreen snorted.

'Then there might be treasure here too,' I said suddenly. 'What if he had robbed a bank, had this room built and hidden the stash somewhere here? Like in the mattress?'

'Don't be idiotic,' Anshu said. 'This is probably just a room someone's built in their basement, maybe to give it on rent or something…'

'And then forgotten all about it?' Nasreen asked.

'Well the person might have died, and not told anyone about this place under his or her house.'

'But why would they need a tunnel leading to the Ridge?' I asked. 'And why would they stock all that food and fancy plates and have a radio receiver and transmitter?'

'If the house above was bombed they wouldn't have been able to get out. That's what the tunnel was for, silly,' Anshu said, frowning. 'So it's most likely a bomb shelter after all; they would need gas masks and a radio to let people know where they were if they got trapped.' She shrugged, 'But the room could have also been given on rent!'

'If we are under someone's house in a basement, then there should be a way up,' I said carefully. 'There should be steps going up and another door.' The others looked at me, and began nodding slowly.

After much indignant sneezing, the dogs had comfortably settled themselves amongst the cushions on the bed. They had certainly made themselves at home.

We gathered around the coffee table. 'You know what,' Anshu said solemnly, 'this would have been so much better a place to live for the Begum of Awadh and her kids than Malcha Mahal.' She looked at me. 'But Umi's right: there should be a door leading out of this room to whatever is built on top of it. Let's find it!'

Well we searched. We spent a good half-hour searching. There was no door anywhere in that room. The walls all round were solid rock: we tapped every inch but never got a hollow sound. We found a couple of small vents, one high up in one corner and the other at near ground level behind the bed.

'What are they for?' I asked.

'Ventilation probably,' Shiv said. 'Hot air escapes via the high vent and cold air comes in through the low one. But they're far too small for anyone to crawl through. Even you, Umi.'

'Very funny!'

'We haven't checked behind the cupboards,' Anshu said, frowning.

Shiv shook his head. 'Wouldn't make sense to have a door there. If the cupboard is right in front of it you can neither get in nor out, especially if you're in a hurry!'

'The cupboards might have a backdoor like in *The Lion, the Witch and the Wardrobe*,' I said. Then I saw the flaw again. 'No, that doesn't work either. You'd still have to upset everything in the cupboard to get in and out.'

Gingerly we sat down on the sofa and chairs, placing our flashlights on the table in front of us. 'Well, it means that the tunnel was the only way in and out of here,' Anshu said slowly. 'So there may not be a house above this room at all.'

I shook my head. 'There has to be a house. It doesn't make sense to have a bomb shelter which you can only reach through a long tunnel in the Ridge. First, you have to go to the Ridge itself, then get to the tunnel entrance at the well and then come all the way here!'

'I'm telling you, it's a spy hideout,' Pankaj said decisively. 'A spy would need all of these things and to use this place as a bolt-hole. He has food, comfort, a kitchen, bathroom and his radio transmitter.' He looked at the vent near the ceiling. 'I bet the antenna or whatever must have been connected through that.'

'Guys, have you noticed anything?' Lavina suddenly said. She'd been pretty quiet so far, just looking around the room wondrously with her big brown eyes.

'What?'

'Well, look at the furniture! It's not the sort of furniture a spy would have. It looks like it's been taken from a millionaire's bedroom. Look at all the wiggly lion legs and carving and gilt paint on them. And look at the bed. It's a four-poster. It all sort of matches with the fancy crockery and cutlery.'

'What's a four-poster?' I asked.

She smiled at me. 'The sort of bed a king or queen would sleep in,' she explained. 'They dress it up with fancy silken drapes and nets like the howdah of a maharaja's elephant.'

'Guys,' Anshu tapped the table for attention. 'We can make this place our secret headquarters; somewhere where we can come to chill out and have a good time. We have electricity and water and a stove and…I mean we could even study here!'

Shiv interrupted. 'You know, if the electricity is on, someone is going to get the bill.'

Anshu grinned. 'We'll cross that bridge when we get to it.' She looked at the weak light. 'Besides, I don't think that bulb uses a lot of power.'

'We can get our own LED bulbs from home,' Pankaj said. 'And light this room up properly. Hey check if the ceiling fan works!'

It did. It started with a hideous creaking screech and then blew down another load of dust all over us. But it worked.

'Man, they don't build things like this anymore,' Shiv said admiringly.

'We can make this room really cozy,' Anshu said. She shook her head and looked around. 'I still can't believe this place. I can bring my guitar here and practice.'

Nasreen got up and walked to the bathroom. 'Let's see if the flush still works,' she grinned. We heard a clanking, clunking sound and squawk from Nasreen and then the sound of water gushing, as she yanked at the chain. The flush was one of those old-fashioned pull-the-chain types that sounded like a knight in armour thrashing around in a drain.

'It does,' she said. 'Now let's see if it fills up again. I want to go!'

And sure enough it did. When Nasreen emerged, she was holding a couple of brooms in her hands. 'I found these in a closet in the bathroom,' she said. 'There are more there. We can clean up this place. Guys, get moving, here you go!'

We cleaned up the room as best we could, and made it look comfortable and cozy. But I was still uneasy. I didn't like unsolved mysteries and this room had one very big one attached to it.

Was it the hideout of a long-dead spy? If so, what kind of a spy had a taste for such fancy and expensive furniture, and who ate tinned food out of fancy plates and silver spoons? That didn't make much sense. And why would a spy need gas masks and helmets? Why would you need gas masks unless you knew there was a risk of getting bombed or gassed? If there was a risk of getting bombed, this room had to have been built underneath another building or house; maybe a very important one. So was it after all, just a bomb shelter? If it was just a bomb shelter where was the door that led to the house or building it was built over? We had searched and found nothing. We had even tapped the ceiling with the brooms thinking there might be a trapdoor but all we heard was a solid 'thunk' of wood on rock, nothing hollow sounding. To make sure we'd also shoved the broom up against the ceiling, just in case the trapdoor—if there was one—was made of stone like a manhole cover. Nothing.

'I don't like it! This is a weird room,' I told Lavina. 'It seems to be a bomb shelter that's been built by ghosts who would just waft in and out of the walls when there was an air-raid.'

'But silly ghosts would be bombproof themselves,' Lavina replied, 'they wouldn't need a shelter in the first place.'

I nodded slowly. 'That exactly is the problem. So what is this place after all?'

Lavina smiled sunnily. 'Let's not worry about that right now. Let's just all enjoy this place while we can. While it's still ours!'

I was still pessimistic and had an uneasy feeling in the pit of my stomach. Lavina was right. I knew we'd be discovered sooner or later, and this hideout would be snatched away from us; adults just couldn't leave kids alone and mind their own beeswax. This room had lain undetected for who knows how many years. But now that we had discovered it, the adult world would not rest until they rumbled us. It was like a law of nature. Like getting old. All we had to do was wait.

Fortunately, or unfortunately, I had no idea at that time of how right I was. Our presence in that room had already been picked up by a couple of listeners. Somewhere not very far away, they had looked at each other, startled; one with its head cocked and the other just listening carefully, a hand behind an ear.

'You heard that too, Golu? What on earth could it be? It sounded like…no but that's not possible at all!'

Then the listener paused and thought a bit.

'Hmm…This is going to be our little secret, okay? If we say anything you know what'll happen. The sky will fall! We'll have to get to the bottom of this ourselves.'

'Okay guys, I think we should head back,' Anshu decided after a while, glancing at her watch. 'It's getting on to lunchtime. We've made some pretty awesome discoveries, I must say.'

'We should check if Khushboo and Salim can come to Malcha Mahal with us today,' Lavina said. 'Like we had told her yesterday.'

When we reached home, we found that Khushboo had beaten us to it.

'There was a call from Khushboo,' Ma informed Anshu. 'She wanted to know if you'd like to go to the Kamala Nehru Ridge in north Delhi for a historical walk with her this evening. She mentioned something about the Flagstaff Tower and Mutiny Memorial and Khooni-Khan jheel.' She smiled fondly at us. 'You'd like to go to a place that's called that, wouldn't you?'

'Thanks Ma, I'll get back to the others and then call her,' Anshu said. She nudged me. 'Go call Pankaj and tell him to ask Salim if he's free this evening. If he says yes then we're on.'

Pankaj got back to me in no time at all. Salim was free and would meet us at the Flagstaff Tower on the Ridge at 4 p.m.

It all fell into place beautifully. Shiv's mom insisted that we go in their Scorpio so we just piled in with our bikes stacked on the roof as Salim followed us on his red Scooty. The only guys who were unhappy were the dogs who we had to leave behind.

It was just too thrilling. That morning we had discovered what could be a spy's den (with an unsolved mystery attached) located deep underground. And here we were playing a dangerous double-agent rendezvous game in real life!

'Well, this second rendezvous was a total success,' Anshu said with a sense of accomplishment after we got back that evening by around 6.30. She was right. The Northern Ridge was far away enough for Khushboo and Salim to be safe from being seen by anyone they knew. It also had good bike trails and lots of benches where girlfriends and boyfriends could sit in peace. Khushboo and Salim disappeared amongst the trees for a long walk saying they'd meet us back at the Flagstaff Tower in an hour, which is what they did. We cycled madly up and down the tarmac road and some of the kuchha tracks, and then sat all in a row on one of the orange benches, drinking water and cooling off. Our own Ridge in central Delhi was wilder and more difficult to cycle in, but this wasn't so bad either. You couldn't really get lost here for very long as you could in our much larger Ridge.

As Khushboo and Salim approached us, Lavina took one look at them and smiled.

'See how happy they look together,' she gushed and I froze because she was sitting next to me and her hot pink cheek was now flush against mine. 'They're meant to be together.' So, I hoped desperately, were we! Pankaj of course had spent nearly all his time looking at the hordes of monkeys that infested the place. Shiv and Anshu were chatting quietly together, and Nasreen was still doing what she called 'cooling down' exercises.

What was really funny was that Khushboo had lectured us about the history of the Red Fort in the car because she had told Vineet that's where she was taking us. In case he asked us questions when we got back, we would have the answers!

But on the way back, Anshu had some questions for Khushboo too: my sister really was a nosey parker.

'So, Didi, when did you first meet Salim Bhai?' she asked innocently.

'When we were in second grade,' Khushboo said, her face splitting into a huge smile. 'He was made to sit next to me so I could teach him C-A-T cat, M-A-T mat, B-A-T bat, R-A-T rat. His spelling was appalling!'

'What?'

'Yes, the teachers decided to put him next to me in the hope his spelling would improve. Also, he was always playing pranks so they hoped that by making him sit next to a girl he'd learn his lesson and stop playing the fool.'

I couldn't imagine Salim playing pranks.

'But isn't Salim Bhai older than you? Then how were you in the same class together?' Anshu asked.

'Yes. He joined school a year late and then, despite my teaching him how to spell cat and bat and rat, was kept behind for a year. So I went ahead.'

'But...but he's studying to be a doctor!' I said. Surely, someone who wants to be a doctor should have been able to spell cat and rat and bat in second grade!

Khushboo smiled. 'Well, I always wanted to be a teacher, and in Salim I found my most challenging pupil. I tutored him all through his school years; I used to go to his house nearly every day. Many times I just wasted my time waiting because he was out on the cricket field, playing. He was crazy about cricket and wanted to become a fast bowler. And he was pretty good too, so no one could say anything to him. He got selected in the school eleven and then for some state-level matches when he was just eighteen. But right from the beginning he knew it wouldn't last: he had a bad ankle that kept giving way. The doctors had said it was a congenital weakness and that he shouldn't strain it. One day, after a bad match, he limped home in a foul mood. I'd been waiting with his sister Saomi. We had Maths scheduled for that day. He stormed into his room and slammed the door. When I went in he was sitting on his bed and I could see he had been crying. I asked him what had happened, fully expecting he'd bite my head off, but he turned to me, his eyes full of tears.

'"What should I do with this wretched ankle, Khush?" he asked. It was swollen pretty badly. "It feels just fine and then suddenly gives way." He was just in grade nine then. So I told him, "You better have a plan B in place. Play for as long as you can and when you have to stop, get ahead with plan B. In one word: study!" After that he put his head down and studied and I think his brain sort of rewired itself too! From the bottom five in class he became one of the top five. Then he was picked for an important Test match. He was on the top of the world. His ankle had been behaving and he had started hoping it had fully recovered.' Khushboo smiled. 'I watched him play on TV. I was more nervous than him, I think. He clean bowled the batsman with his very first ball. The wickets went all over the place.' She shook her head. 'The idiot was so thrilled he leapt about four feet high and landed smack on that wretched ankle...And that was it. He stopped playing after that Test appearance. But I guess he knew he was good enough for the top level and that was enough. And he never gave up cricket entirely. He coaches you boys. He wants to be a doctor specializing in sports injuries.'

'His parents didn't mind you coming over every day to give him tuition?' Nasreen asked.

'Not at all! They called me beti and were so grateful. They said I was the only person he really listened to.'

'And your parents? Didn't they know? Or mind?'

'Yes, they knew. They thought I was teaching Saomi!'

'So how...how did you...' Anshu nodded expressively and turned a bit pink.

'Well dear, what I liked most about Salim was that he didn't for a moment object to my teaching or bullying or lecturing him even though I was younger than him, and yet a year *senior* to him in class. Very few boys would accept or stomach that, but he did and with a big silly grin on his face. He actually listened to me.' She grinned and went on: 'And, I took full advantage of that: I would pull his ears and rap his knuckles and sometimes be really mean to him and he'd just take it.'

Oh-oh, I thought, that was so much like Shiv and Anshu.

'I bet that was because he fell madly in love with you from the moment you sat next to him in second grade,' Lavina grinned.

'Maybe! He did show me and teach me a lot of beautiful things, too. Like…one time he showed me this enormous gross caterpillar that was bingeing its head off and getting fatter and fatter. It was revolting!

'"Just see what happens," he told me. One day the caterpillar stopped eating and spun itself a silk cocoon. And then a week later, Salim called me down very early in the morning. He showed me the jam jar in which we had kept the cocoon, and said, "Watch!"

'An hour later, this gorgeous dappled butterfly unfolded itself from the chrysalis and hung its wings out to dry before flying off.

'"Isn't it amazing?" he told me, "that from something so gross and greedy something so beautiful and ethereal can emerge? All this butterfly will now ever eat is nectar." I grinned and told him, "So there's hope for you yet."

'Another time he took me off to Malcha Mahal and said wasn't it sad that some people thought they were so much superior to others and also that surely the Government was stonehearted to make such proud people live there, in a "mahal" which was decrepit and ruined. It was like the reverse of the butterfly thing.'

'So his parents didn't object to you being friends with him?' Nasreen suddenly asked.

'Not at all! But later Mama and Papa and that fool Vineet did and still do.' She looked at Nasreen. 'Honestly, I can't say that Salim's parents simply thought it was safer to let Mama and Papa do the objecting... but I don't think so: they've been so sweet and kind to me all the time! They used to tell me, "Beti, you've made our beta a first class first!"'

'Will...will you change your religion if you marry Salim Bhai?' Anshu blurted and went very red. 'Sorry...'

Khushboo shook her head. 'No. Why should I? And for that matter why should Salim change his religion? Why can't we be just the way we are?'

'Wow,' Pankaj suddenly piped up. 'I never knew

Salim Bhai was interested in caterpillars and butterflies. I wonder if he likes spiders and scorpions too!'

Vineet did buttonhole us after we got back. He'd made it a habit to lie in wait for me and Anshu in the stairwell of our block and then would accost us suddenly. It was a bit unnerving; he was quite an ugly hulk and his yellow teeth glimmered scarily in the dim light.

'So what did you see, and did Khushboo meet anyone?' he asked straight out. 'Did she borrow any of your phones to make a call?'

'Oh, she talked about the Diwan-e-Aam and the Diwan-e-Khas and how the British cleared the land in front of the fort and built those hideous barracks inside...' Anshu started off glibly. 'No, she didn't meet or talk to anyone except us. You know she hates being disturbed when she's taking a class.'

'Hmm...I see, very good. Umm...does she talk about anyone else when she's with you? Like that Salim fellow or anyone else?'

'No!' Anshu said with wide innocent eyes. 'Should she?'

'No! She daren't!' Vineet said belligerently. 'That useless fellow has been following her and trying to pull her dupatta ever since she was in school.'

'Oh,' Anshu said feigning surprise. 'Did she

complain or something? Is he stalking her? She could complain to the police if she's being harassed.'

Vineet glared at us probably realizing he had said too much. 'Just forget it,' he grunted. 'I can deal with him myself if required, no need for any police rubbish. But if you see him anywhere near her, inform me straight way.'

'Sure, Vineet,' we said together in a tone which would have put Ma on an all-points hyper-alert. Happily we pocketed the 500-rupee note he handed us. More pizza and ice creams for us all, which maybe we could enjoy in our newly discovered spy nest.

The next morning, while waiting for the school bus, Shiv asked the question we all ought to have asked right at the beginning:

Why didn't Khushboo and Salim simply go to a court and get married and be done with it? Then there'd be no need for all this cloak-and-dagger, hush-hush stuff (which was exciting nonetheless) and they could be happily with each other. That evening when we went for tuition (this time a normal home-tuition), Anshu asked Khushboo just that.

'We don't want to get married right now,' Khushboo said. 'Salim needs to finish his MBBS and I want to complete my PhD and begin to teach. There's no hurry!'

'So you'll have to wait until then at least,' Anshu said.

Khushboo nodded. 'I guess.' She pursed her lips. 'Except that Papa and Vineet have already lined up Biker for me. His family is very rich, you see.'

'You can marry who you want,' Anshu said hotly. 'You don't have to marry that creep.'

Khushboo's face went red, too, with anger. 'It's worse than that. They're planning my wedding for April or May. So Salim and I might just *have* to get married before that!'

That meant this cloak-and-dagger spy game we were playing would have to continue at least till then. We were in for exciting if not dangerous times. And there was also the matter of the mystery bomb-shelter. Suddenly our lives seemed a bit too exciting to be real!

7

I was setting off for coaching the next evening, when at the bottom of the stairs I was brought to a jarring halt by someone calling harshly:

'Oye, you! Dada!'

Who the heck was calling the dog? It sounded like…Sure enough, Vineet stepped out of the shadowy stairwell. Just in time I remembered that I had told him that my name was Dada. Even so my heart was sinking as I walked up to where he stood, his fingers casually looped in the pockets of his jeans. Was he going to search my kitbag where a letter from Khushboo was safely tucked away?

'You know, I've paid you a lot of money and so far you haven't come back with anything. Zero!' He looked at me dispassionately. I felt like a mosquito he could swat at any moment.

'But sir, Khushboo Didi hasn't spoken to anyone or met anyone when she's with us.'

He nodded. 'Maybe! But now I want you to get information from that Salim fellow.'

'Information? What kind of information? He just coaches us.'

'I want to know what he does other than that. What he likes and doesn't like. Does he have a girlfriend? Where does he like to hang out?'

I gulped. 'Sir, he coaches us. That would sound rude and he may get angry.'

Vineet suddenly had me by the collar. 'Abbe, just do it, okay?' he grated. 'Ask him! And then report back to me, got it? It will be better for you!' Then he let me go. His eyes were like black stones. I stepped back and blinked.

'Yes,' I said, quietly feeling my neck. His grip had been like a manacle. This fellow was dangerous.

'Good, now we understand each other. Ring me after your coaching class.'

Of course I didn't ask Salim anything of the sort, I didn't have to. We all knew very well that he had a girlfriend. But after coaching I had to ring Vineet and give him the feedback. I think I was smart in how I handled the situation.

'Hello? Vineet sir? This is er…Dada.'

'Did you speak to the bugger? Did you ask him?'

'He got angry and said I should focus on my cricket and not ask stupid personal questions.'

'So he didn't answer your question?'

'He said whether he had a girlfriend or not was none of my business.'

'Very well. Okay then, this is what you'll have to do. I want you and that other fellow who goes for coaching with you to keep tabs on him. Where does he go after coaching? What does he do during the day?'

'Sir, that would be difficult. We have school all day. He had said he's studying to be a doctor so studies all day.'

'He must go out at some time. If you or your friends see him leave, follow him… Check if he really goes to the library. Which one?'

'He has a Scooty and we only have bicycles. He must go to his college or university library, I suppose.'

Vineet made an exasperated noise. 'Then just take an auto and follow him! I'll pay you! Pretend this is a great spy game that you're playing and that he is your main suspect. You can do this on weekends. Do you understand? It will be better for you.'

Bah and no can do. On weekends we'd be cycling to our own personal secret headquarters deep underground, which, ironically, had also perhaps once been a den for spies. And then of course we had to fix up what Lavina had called the, 'secret trysts' between Salim and Khushboo. But I had to be careful now. This guy was threatening me again.

'Okay, I'll try. But on weekends Mama and Papa usually take us out or we go cycling and then Khushboo Didi takes us out for historical walks. But I'll try.'

'You'd better! Ring me when you have something.' He banged the phone down.

Anshu, Lavina, Nasreen and Shiv all had big gun exams coming up (their Class X Boards) in March so they now went to Khushboo for tuition every day after school. So everyday there would be a letter, and sometimes a small packet for me to deliver to Salim either directly or through Pankaj who lived in his block.

At the cricket nets, Shiv and I had recently been joined by a new guy. Salim had noticed him standing at the edge of the park, watching us being put through our paces by him. He always had a cricket bat with him and plainly looked like he wanted to join us; he had a longing, hangdog look. So one day Salim just went up to him and spoke to him. The boy said his name was Raghav that he was new to the area. He lived a couple of streets away and was mad about cricket. He was a stocky fellow and had a long face like a basset hound and glistening black hair and slightly protuberant eyes. He came on a bicycle and obviously had recently fallen off his bicycle judging by the bruises on his cheeks. Salim had a short tête-à-tête with him and then brought him along to meet us, saying he would now be joining us. Salim is just like that—a sucker for hard-luck stories. Raghav had obviously told Salim that he was crazy about cricket and wanted to excel in it but had no one to guide him.

'Okay, let's see how good you are now,' Salim said and asked me to bowl to him. Raghav was solid in defence, blocking everything I threw at him with good technique.

'Okay,' Salim agreed after the session. 'You can join in too. Ask them about the timings and don't be late.'

'Thank you, sir,' Raghav looked delighted and mournful at the same time.

He turned up for his first coaching session armed with a shiny new kitbag, pads, gloves, bat et al: better kitted out than Shiv and I. Shiv was a bit put out at first, but soon realized that it could be useful to have another person batting at the other end. And I realized that it was better to have to bowl to different types of batsmen than simply one—Shiv—whose strengths and weaknesses I knew inside out. Raghav seemed quite friendly if a bit reserved with a faraway kind of look in his eye, but we quickly warmed to him.

The days sped by: it became foggy and cold as winter took hold, and this made our weekend forays to the secret step-well and underground chamber all the more exciting. There was no question of swimming in the well now, but we had made our underground lair very comfortable indeed, bringing new, colourful cushions, a small gas cylinder, and books and games. We'd put new bulbs into the sockets so it was now cheerfully and brightly lit and Shiv had brought his old boom-box too, so we had music. Anshu had brought her guitar here several times and practiced her solo numbers before we all joined in, in a jam session. Or Nasreen, who really had a husky sexy voice, would sing and give us all goosebumps. Anshu and the others would even study here all through Sundays, while Pankaj probed the corners for his beloved spiders and other creepy crawlies which he would proudly show to Nasreen. We'd left the rusting food tins in the cupboards alone as also the gas masks and helmets (which were big and uncomfortable). But we ate and drank out of fancy bone china, and with knives and forks that after polishing with Silvo (Nasreen's idea) turned out to be 'Sterling' silver! From some place called Sheffield in England! Of course, at the back of our minds there was always the question of whose shelter this was, and was there a house above it and if so how the hell did anyone get down here or get up there? And of course, the big question: would the landlord turn up one day and ask us just what we thought we were doing in his private World War II bomb-shelter?

We would have been extremely perturbed had we

known that our chatter and music were being regularly listened to by the two secret listeners. But they kept their counsel and told no one about the strange noises and laughter they were hearing from time to time. And soon they seemed to know that we'd be there on the weekends, especially Sundays.

The weekends were always exciting because we went on 'historical walks' with Khushboo. We had visited Purana Quila, the Zoo, Rajghat, Humayun's Tomb, Qutub Minar, and even Tughlakabad. Not to mention a couple of multiplexes when they wanted to see movies together and even malls when they just wanted to stroll around and chill like everyone else. These were risky, but so far we and they'd been lucky: there had been no emergencies.

'Look at them,' Lavina would gush after every outing. 'They're more in love with each other than ever before.' And her big brown eyes would get all dreamy and gooey and I would stare at her mesmerized. Then she would smile at me and gently squeeze my hand completely making my day.

Around the first week of March, Vineet finally gave up on us. He ambushed Anshu and me near the stairwell again one evening, after we had just returned from a 'historical' outing to the Garden of Five Senses, which actually was really notorious for canoodling couples. When we told him, yet again, that no, Khushboo had met no one and made no calls, he just folded his arms across his chest and sneered at us.

'Very well then, listen. I'm not paying you anything until you have the information I need.'

'But she's not seeing anyone when she talks to us!' Anshu said earnestly. Literally, I suppose that was the truth as any lawyer would see it! When Khushboo lectured us in the car or in the Metro she only talked about the historical place we were supposed to be going to. 'She just talks to us about history and archaeology and interesting stuff like that. She knows so much!'

'And sir, there's nothing to report on the Salim Bhai front either,' I said. 'He is studying or goes to the library late in the evenings. Shiv and I have to be home by then. He said he's coaching us to reduce his stress.'

Vineet's eyes suddenly glittered. 'Hmph!' he snorted. 'But if I find out you are lying, you will regret it for the rest of your lives,' he threatened and stalked off, glowering. Anshu looked at me and took my hand.

'It's okay, Umi, he's just trying to spook us,' she said, not sounding too convinced. 'But thank God he's off our backs. He's a piece of work, isn't he?'

What was quite disconcerting was that now Biker was nearly always present when we went to Khushboo's for tuition. And in spite of the weekend trysts with Salim and the daily exchange of letters, she was beginning to look strained and tense again.

I was there one afternoon, (now reading Alexander Dumas' *The Three Musketeers* and really enjoying it) when the doorbell rang. It was a delivery boy with a large packet. Khushboo's mother and Vineet (lounging about in front of the TV as usual) took the parcel.

'Your wedding cards have arrived!' Khushboo's mother trilled, rushing up to the dining table. Vineet ripped open the parcel. Khushboo had gone completely ashen, but then her eyes glittered angrily. All of us just stared with our mouths open.

The card was large and ornate in turquoise blue and gold and silver and embossing and all that. The date for the wedding had been set for the beginning of May— not very sensible considering it would be the height of summer. The groom, of course, was Kanwar 'Biker' Balvinder Asthana who was now standing behind his bride-to-be, squeezing her shoulders and grinning like a ruddy baboon—though I think that would be insulting to the baboon.

'Oh!' Khushboo said and shook her head. 'Oh!' She shook her head again. Vineet watched her like a hawk, Biker looked at her stupidly.

'What?' Vineet asked harshly. 'What's the matter?'

'I've told you I don't want to get married just yet,' Khushboo said in a level voice.

In a flash Vineet slapped her. 'Shut up!' he shouted.

'You'll get married on 2nd May and that's the end of it!'

The Biker goon just watched with his arms across his chest. By god, if he cared an iota for Khushboo, he should have been tearing out Vineet's throat.

Their father, in a crumpled kurta-pajama, entered the room yawning. He was a big, burly man with a bushy white moustache and uncombed white hair, and reminded me of what the yeti might look like.

'What's all this?' he asked truculently.

'The wedding cards have been delivered, ji!' Khushboo's mother said showing him one.

'Very good! Are they all right? The fellow charged an arm and a leg for them.'

'Papa, I don't want to get married just yet. I want to do my PhD first. I have said this many times already.' Khushboo's voice was still calm. 'And I don't…love… Biker!' she went on defiantly.

Her father stormed up to the table.

'Again this PhD nonsense? You will do as you're told! Do you understand? Are you still running after that Muslim trash? You go near him or speak to him or think about him and we'll kill you with our bare hands. Understand?'

Around the table we exchanged stricken glances. Both Vineet and their father stood over Khushboo, their fists clenching and unclenching. She would have been properly beaten up if we hadn't been there. I glanced furtively at them and suddenly I was really scared. When Papa lost his temper with either Anshu or me, his eyes would flash fire but then in no time at all he'd calm down and be all over us hugging and kissing and offering to take us out to the movies. But here, there was total hatred and contempt in Khushboo's father's eyes: he and Vineet would not hesitate to seriously harm her if she disobeyed them. Her stupid mother just looked on with a prissy, martyred expression on her face.

Khushboo calmly closed the book she had been reading from. 'Children, I think we'll continue with this tomorrow,' she said.

Anshu looked at her as we began collecting our notebooks and pens. 'Okay Didi, is there any homework you'd like to give us?'

Khushboo glanced quickly at her family. Vineet and her father had moved away and were poring over the wedding card and exclaiming how 'sundar' it looked, cooling down no doubt. Even Biker had joined them.

'Dear, just go over what we covered today and attempt one of the Test papers that I set you,' Khushboo said, 'here, I'll write it out for you.' She tore a page out of her pad and carefully wrote something on it. Then she folded it and handed it over to Anshu. 'Put it in the envelope, please,' she whispered quietly, glancing at her family. Anshu nodded. The day's usual love-letter was already safely in her knapsack. Usually that was the first thing Khushboo handed over, but now there was an addition. No problem for my bindas sister, she just coolly took out the envelope, carefully opened it, put in the new note and re-sealed it.

I handed Salim the letter the next evening and then Shiv told him straight out:

'Sir, yesterday we were at Khushboo Didi's place for tuition as usual when the wedding cards were delivered. She is supposed to marry that Biker. They've set the date for 2nd May.'

Salim tried to look normal but I could see he was taken aback. 'Er...and how did Khushboo react?' he asked.

'I think she was stunned, sir,' Shiv said.

'And very angry,' I added. 'She was upset. Her brother hit her in front of all of us.'

'Oh!' Salim hooded his eyes. 'Very well! Should we get on with warming up exercises now?' And I wondered what he'd write in his letter to her today. Matters were beginning to heat up. A deadline had been set. Then Raghav sailed up on his bike and the coaching session began in earnest.

As usual, Salim had his reply ready by the end of the session. He'd made us run around the park six times and that's when he sat down to write it. He slipped it to me and I nodded.

'Bhai, did she mention the invitation?' I asked. He nodded.

'Yes, thanks. It's okay Umesh, we'll just have to get married before that and go away.'

Shiv and Raghav were in the midst of a conversation as I joined them after having tucked away the letter safely.

'Umm, I don't know,' Shiv was saying, sounding doubtful. 'You see it's like this: we have this gang and I'll have to ask the others...'

I looked quizzically at him. 'Raghav wants to come biking with us,' Shiv explained.

'My parents won't let me cycle alone on the streets,' Raghav explained. 'I've seen you guys and those dogs take off for long rides. You come back after ages. I don't think my parents will object if I come along with you.'

I exchanged glances with Shiv and looked at Raghav. His cheek bruises had faded but now his lips seemed swollen. Another fall? Just how good a cyclist was he if he kept falling off his bike? 'Raghav, Shiv is right: we'll have to ask the others. It's a sort of gang convention.' I pointed at his lip. 'You got that falling off your cycle? And those bruises that you had earlier?'

Raghav was about to deny it and then looked

sheepish and nodded, obviously thinking he'd better level with us. 'Yes, I wasn't quite watching where I was going.' He shrugged and sighed. 'Okay, ask your gang members and let me know what you guys decide!'

'Well?' I asked Shiv as we made our way back home. 'If we let him come along it'll mean letting him into the gang. Do you think we should?'

Shiv grinned. 'We'll have to ask the bosses,' he said good-naturedly, 'Your sister and Nasreen!'

'He seems like an okay guy,' I said, 'Doesn't seem to have any hang-ups.'

'Yeah, but we've got these top-secret hideouts we go to,' Shiv went on. 'Plus we're into this spying business and covering up...we're deep, man!'

'Maybe he won't be so keen after we've taken him on one of our cross-country rides through the Ridge,' I said, grinning. 'Especially if he keeps falling off his bike. And we don't have to show him the step-well or bomb-shelter of course.'

'Well, we'll check with the others and maybe take a vote.'

We broached the subject with the others on our next visit to our secret den that weekend. It was now approaching the middle of March and earlier that winter we'd made our bomb shelter even cozier by smuggling in a rod heater. Thankfully the electrical circuits didn't blow when we switched it on and we (especially Lavina and Pankaj) had happily huddled around it. Now we could use it to toast sandwiches and heat rotis!

'What?' Anshu said suspiciously, when we told them about Raghav later that day at the hideout. 'So this guy has been coming for coaching to Salim but now he wants to come biking with us too?'

'Yes!'

Anshu looked around. 'What do you think guys?'

Lavina raised her eyebrows. 'How long have you known him for?'

'A little over a month. So far he's never missed a single session. He seems very keen. He's a bit on the quiet side.'

'He has a decent bike too,' I added.

'Hmm…' Anshu said, 'Nas, what do you think?'

'We could give him a trial sort of thing,' Nasreen said slowly. 'He may be good at cricket but can he bike?'

'That's what I thought,' I said. 'He seems to fall off quite often judging by his bruises. We take him for a few trial rides to the Ridge and see how he fares.'

'But we'll have to be careful,' Pankaj said suddenly. 'We'll have to be careful about what we say in his presence. We can't talk about Khushboo and Salim when he's around, or about this place. He's going to cramp our style.'

Shiv looked a bit troubled. 'You know, so far there's

no reason for us to refuse to let him come biking with us, at least. He seems to be a pretty decent sort. He's not obnoxious or conceited or anything like that. It would seem so mean of us to say, no way, you can't join us! Put yourself in his shoes: he says he's new to the area and doesn't seem to have any friends…'

Anshu smiled at Shiv. 'You're such a soft teddy-bear, goofball,' she teased. She went on decisively. 'Okay! We'll take him on a couple of cross-country rides and take a call from there. If he bonds well with us, we'll consider his joining the gang properly. But yes, until then we'll have to be careful of what we say in his presence. Agreed?'

We all nodded.

'You know, there's just one thing we really have to watch out for,' Anshu said suddenly as we helped ourselves to the giant pizza we had brought along. 'Just keep your fingers crossed that this guy doesn't ask if he can join us for tuitions with Khushboo. That would really put the cat amongst the pigeons!' She looked at me. 'Umi, which school does he go to anyway? He's not in ours certainly.'

I told her.

'Do you know if he's good in studies?'

I shook my head. 'We only meet for cricket coaching.'

'Okay, so we go easy on the tuition talk too.' She

shook her head suddenly. 'Man, this guy is already cramping our style!'

'I don't think he'll want to join tuitions: it's a bit late for that now,' I said.

And then of course, I nearly went and blew it! We were having catch practice: Salim was whacking the ball at us making us dive left and right or jump up high. We had to be alert because we didn't know who he'd be aiming at. Well, he hit the ball towards me and I dived acrobatically and got my fingers to it before snapping them away with a cry of pain. It had been a hard whack and the ball had smashed into my fingernail making it bleed.

'Are you all right?' Salim asked, walking up as I looked at my dripping finger bemused and a bit stunned.

'Yes…yes sir,' I said doubtfully. 'Sir, I have a first-aid kit in my bag,' I said, holding my hand up to slow the bleeding. 'It has gauze bandages, sticking plaster and antiseptic.'

'Raghav, go and fetch it, please,' Salim said.

Too late I remembered that Khushboo's letter was also tucked away safely right next to the pouch in my bag. I hadn't been able to hand it over to Salim yet and had thought I'd do so when he sent us to run around the park or once Raghav left. And Khushboo had started getting careless because she would inscribe her pink or lilac envelopes with 'To My Dearest, Darling Salim, from your sweetest Khushboo' in fancy twirly handwriting and would decorate it with hearts and mushy stuff like that. Raghav was sure to see it!

'Found it?' I yelled, getting up and running towards the bag as Shiv and Salim looked at me in surprise.

'Ya, I got it, thanks,' Raghav said quietly, looking up from the bag. He held it up. 'This is it, isn't it, with the red cross?'

I could only hope that it had been too dark at the bottom of my bag for him to have read anything on that envelope. And in future I would have to tell Khushboo to leave her envelopes blank. At any rate he probably didn't know who Khushboo was, so what did it matter even if he had seen the envelope?

One Sunday in late March we were down in our secret bomb shelter as usual, when I suddenly thought of something. It had become quite warm, and we were now looking forward to swimming in the step-well. The Ridge looked quite fresh and green with new leaves everywhere and trees in flower. But soon it would be dry, dusty and desiccated. The gang 'seniors' had just two more papers to finish and that's what suddenly made me realize something, which none of the others had obviously thought about.

'Hey guys,' I told them as they sprawled around our little room cramming. 'What do we do after your exams?'

Anshu looked at me and frowned. 'What do you mean? We can come here and chill and swim and have a great time.'

'Sure, but we won't be going for tuitions after the exams. So how will Khushboo and Salim exchange letters? How will we fix up outings?'

'Oh! It never struck me!' Anshu said. 'We'd better think of something.'

'Tuitions after the exams are a no-no,' Shiv said decisively. 'But we can still go on our historical field trips. We can just say that we find them very interesting and that as Khushboo is a history-whiz, we'd like it if she can continue taking us.'

'I guess it could work,' Anshu said. 'Anyway, we'd better tell them.'

When I told Salim this he nodded.

'Don't worry, I've thought of a way out,' he said, smiling. 'I'll be buying her a phone soon. I'll give it to you to give to her when I get it. Then there'll be no need for letters anymore. It'll get you guys off the hook too, you've been taking a huge risk for us and that's been bothering us no end.'

'But she'll still have to fix up the outings with us,' I said. 'Otherwise she won't be allowed to come out of the house.'

A frown creased his forehead. 'I suppose so,' he agreed, 'but at least the daily risk will be reduced a lot.'

How big that risk was, was brought home to us on our very next field visit. The Board exams were done and we'd planned a celebratory 'historical' walk to the Sundar Nursery, which has some old monuments that had been recently 'revamped'. It was also a big enough place for Khushboo and Salim to walk about in with a bit of privacy. We were on our way in Shiv's Scorpio when I noticed the dirt bike behind us! Biker was driving with Vineet pillion. Clearly, they were following us.

'Guys, we'd better change our destination. We're being followed,' I said urgently.

'What?' was the clamorous reaction from the gang.

'This is what we've got to do,' I said, thinking furiously. 'You guys get dropped off at the zoo. I'll duck down and stay in the car, and Surinder Uncle (the driver) can take me to Sundar Nursery. I'll meet Salim there and tip him off.' I frowned. 'Then I'll come back and collect you. You guys come out in an hour's time. Really we ought to force our parents to get us phones!'

Anshu looked at me. 'Good thinking, Umi,' she said. 'So we just continue on our walk with Khushboo and those two fellows can follow us all they want round and round the monkeys' cages!'

'I just hope they don't realize that you're not amongst us,' Lavina said and man, yet again I felt this huge rush of woozy love for her: she'd been thinking about me!

'Don't worry,' I whispered. 'I'll keep an eye out: we'll have to think of something if they too split up and one of them follows you and the other me. But I'll duck down so that the car will appear to be empty.'

'Khushboo Didi, did you tell Vineet that we'd be going to Sundar Nursery?' Anshu asked. 'If you did, he might wonder why we're going to the zoo instead…'

'That won't matter too much,' Nasreen said. 'They'll probably stick to following Khushboo Didi. If they suspect something she's the one they'll follow. They want to see where she goes and who she's meeting, not us!'

'Yes,' I said slowly. 'They could have reached there independently—no need to follow us if they knew where we were going. But I think they do suspect something and think it'll be better if they followed us just to make sure we're going where we said we'd be going.' I grinned. 'Which, at the moment we're not! So they must be pretty pleased that they decided to follow us. Their suspicious are being validated. Except that they'll find that we're going for an innocent walk to the zoo instead, after all!'

'Sorry Khushboo Didi, your tryst today has been wrecked,' Lavina said as though she were to blame.

'It's all right, dear. It's much better this way. We can always set up another meeting.'

Chattering noisily the rest of the gang and Khushboo got off at the gates of the zoo, as I ducked low in the Scorpio and told Surinder Uncle to take me to Sundar Nursery. He was hugely amused by all this cloak-and-dagger stuff and grinned genially. To my great relief, Vineet and Biker seemed to have decided to stick like burrs to the others. They parked the bike near a popcorn vendor, had a quick word with him (to keep an eye on the bike probably) and made off for the ticket counter. At Sundar Nursery, I met Salim at the entrance and told him what had happened.

'Thanks,' he said quietly patting my head. 'That was quick thinking!'

'You'd better get her that phone quickly,' I said. 'It'll be so much easier. Okay, bye, I'm going back to the zoo to pick them up.'

I had to lie low at the zoo for about half an hour. First I scanned the parking lot and saw the dirt bike, angled stylishly amongst other bikes, near the popcorn vendor's stall. So they were still here. The zoo had begun emptying out now and there were droves of people emerging and getting into their cars or onto their bikes and scooters and even buses. Taking advantage of the hustle and bustle, I slipped out of the Scorpio and drifted nonchalantly towards the bike. The popcorn vendor was busy serving hungry customers. Casually I went right up to the bike, as if to admire it. Then I slipped out my penknife and stabbed it viciously into the bike's rear tyre, jamming it in and then yanking it out. I darted quickly away as the tyre hissed shrilly as it deflated and joined the bustling crowd in front of the vendor. Damn, he heard the sudden hiss and looked up, but I kept my wits about me and raising my hand yelled '*Oye bhaiyya, ek popcorn*!' to divert his attention. I bought my bag and returned happily to the car. The gang and Khushboo emerged shortly and we were on our way.

'They followed us all the way,' Anshu reported as we set off. She giggled. 'They pretended to be very interested in animals!' She peered through the back of the Scorpio. 'Are they still following us?'

I grinned. 'I don't think so—not yet. Biker's bike had this unexpected puncture you see, they must be attending to that.'

At our next coaching session Salim handed me a little box.

'This is the mobile,' he said softly. 'It's been set up. All she has to do is use it. It's got quite a few apps—WhatsApp, etc., so she shouldn't have a problem. And both of you, thank you so much for what you've done for us. We owe you big time!'

'No problem, sir, it was great fun,' I chuckled. 'Smuggling letters in and out under that Vineet's nose!'

'Umesh, you all be careful. He's dangerous!'

'We will be.'

We could see that Khushboo was thrilled when we handed over the mobile to her at our next—and final—class.

'He's set it up; it's ready for use. He said to take care that you're not overheard by anyone while talking to him,' I said, hooding my eyes secret-agent style. 'And not to keep in lying around.'

'Thank you, kids,' Khushboo said, with tears in her eyes. 'I don't know what we would have done without you guys.'

8

'So where should we go?' I asked the gang as we gathered with our bikes and the dogs in the colony park early next morning, awaiting Raghav.

'We can take him to the polo ground and some of the trails around it,' Shiv said.

'You know, we haven't been back to Malcha Mahal for a while,' Anshu said. 'I really would like to go back there.'

'Isn't that one of our secret destinations?' Pankaj asked.

'Well, it's hardly secret. I mean, there were what, something like three hundred people there the last time we went,' Anshu pointed out.

'We could take him there via some of the inside trails, not the main Bistadari road,' I said. 'Just to see how good he is at cross-country biking.'

Anshu grinned. 'You know we really must take Khushboo and Salim there,' she said. 'After all, it's the place that kick-started our great interest in Delhi's history!'

We grinned. She had a point!

Raghav showed up punctually and we set off but were stopped by the cops at a major road-crossing, beyond which was the Ridge, because some VIP was to pass. They looked at us and the dogs who had sat down obediently on Nasreen's command grinning as always, and raised their eyebrows, but said nothing. One of them even smiled, which sort of zapped us. Then we heard the sirens.

'The cops really behave as if they've got ants in their pants when a VIP passes by,' Lavina remarked as we waited.

'Wonder who it could be?' Nasreen said. 'Ah here he comes!'

Actually, we could see the convoy approach from quite a distance away. First, two motorcycle outriders and Police Gypsies and jeeps came streaming down, their sirens screaming and lights flashing. They were followed by two huge black Mercedes Benz (with tinted windows) followed by a comet's tail of emergency vehicles, cars and SUVs. But then a weird thing happened. As they approached our crossing, one of the Mercs suddenly slowed, causing the vehicles behind to cram on their brakes. The poor cops looked stunned, frozen as they saluted. The Merc passed us at just about

40 kmph and then zoomed off again—and everyone heaved a sigh of relief.

'Wow! Did you see that? They slowed right down as they passed us! What was that about?' I asked, turning to Shiv. He, with this cheesy ear-to-ear grin, was standing to attention at the edge of the crossing and had snapped a smart military salute as the VIP car had passed us by.

'Man, that was awesome! How did you know it was the President? You made the President of India's motorcade slow down for you!' and we all began ragging him. 'It's easy,' Shiv explained. 'I know what the President's limo looks like! I check out all the videos about her on YouTube.'

We all knew that Shiv was a big fan of Mary Kom the boxer, and Sakshi Malik the wrestler. He was thrilled, when just recently our second lady President was elected.

Dr Ayushi Khandelwal was much like the late Dr Abdul Kalam, who had loved and encouraged kids so much. She was quite an extraordinary woman. I mean, the lady had climbed Everest when she was very young and was a complete computer whiz. She had built her own computer and other gadgets! She was a qualified surgeon, too. If Dr APJ Kalam had been known as the 'People's President', she was known as the 'Children's President'. She had once famously said, 'There's nothing more important than our children'! She loved springing surprise visits to schools because she was an ardent believer that education was the way to go.

Shiv never tired of reading up about her—what she had said, tweeted, announced through the day. And would often feed us various tidbits of the information he gathered. So of course he was thrilled that she had seen him, even though he had only guessed that it was her in the giant Mercedes-Benz that had passed us.

'You know, my dad said that when he was a kid, he and his friends were waiting outside their colony for Jawaharlal Nehru to pass by so they could wave at him,' Pankaj said. 'And guess what, Nehruji leaned out of his jeep and threw them a bunch of roses as he went past!'

'Nehruji was so handsome,' Lavina sighed. 'Not like the creeps we have today. They don't even shave every day.'

'But naturally,' Nasreen retorted, 'their normal habitat should be jail, so what do you expect?'

'Come on guys, let's move!' Anshu leant over the handlebars and we were off. Raghav did fine. He kept up with us easily, even though he now had bruises on his calves; the guy probably had thin veins and arteries I thought, or thin blood. We rattled and bumped through rocky trails, had to swerve and duck to avoid keekar twigs scattered around and eye-level branches— and physically push our bikes through impenetrable bits. He didn't mind any of it and just seemed so grateful that we'd included him in our expedition.

'This is just great,' he kept saying, 'thanks for having me along!'

'No problem, Raghav,' Anshu said. 'You're a pretty decent biker.'

He was astonished by Malcha Mahal that was thankfully deserted again. We sat down to rest with the panting dogs arrayed around us. It was quiet and peaceful except for one bird that let loose with a loud ringing kutroo-kutroo-kutroo call, soon to be joined by another farther off.

'They're brown-headed barbets,' Pankaj informed us. 'They love the summer. They're green and can be difficult to spot. But they look like idiots!'

'I still can't get over how those poor people lived here for so many years,' Anshu said, shielding her eyes as a sudden gust of wind blew. We all exchanged glances: I knew we were all wishing we were at our step-well or in the depths of our cool secret World War II shelter.

'So you've shifted here recently?' I asked Raghav, thinking it was time we cross-examined him a bit before letting him become a full-fledged member of our gang. He nodded.

'Yes,' he said, 'I used to live in Mumbai earlier. Then my parents separated and my mom came here.'

'Any brothers and sisters?' Lavina asked. He shook

his head. Suddenly his face closed up and he looked at the floor.

'What does your mom do?' Pankaj asked idly, using a stick to pick up a shiny black ant that had a gigantic head. 'Just look at this guy! He's a solider.'

'Umm…my dad lives in Mumbai and she…' Raghav mumbled.

Lavina's lovely eyes grew big. 'Oh poor guy, he must be so torn between his parents,' she whispered to me. I loved the feel of her soft lips brushing my ear.

'Yeah,' I whispered back and then saw Nasreen grinning at us and winking. (Thank god she didn't blow her football referee whistle!) Anshu and Shiv were talking softly together, looking at the forest outside. Pankaj was studying his ant with a 10X magnifier.

'Oh so your mom is a single parent,' Lavina said. 'I have so many friends whose parents have separated.'

Raghav shot her a grateful look and I felt the first twinge of jealousy. He nodded.

'Actually mom met this person through Facebook and…' he shrugged and looked doleful, '…and now we're here.'

'Oh!' Lavina didn't know where to look, poor thing.

'You seem to bruise very easily,' I said, changing the subject. 'Those are nasty contusions on your calves.' I'd recently come across the word 'contusion', which means a gash-like bruise, and wanted to use it. Raghav looked down at his legs and nodded. 'I guess,' he said, quietly.

We returned home by lunchtime. It was beginning to get hot and I could sense that the gang was just itching to set off again afterwards for the step-well. We said bye to Raghav and gathered around the stairwell. Anshu grinned mischievously.

'Okay guys, here's the thing,' she said. 'We stay at home like good children till 4 o'clock and then head for the step-well. Bring your swimsuits and towels, we'll have our inaugural swim today.' Her black eyes gleamed. 'I'm also going to speak to Khushboo on her new phone. Just suggest that maybe she could take us all for a historical walk through the Ridge to Malcha Mahal sometime...where, hey presto Salim will just happen to be waiting for her.' She looked at Pankaj and me. 'You guys get on the line to Salim and ask him!'

Lavina nodded excitedly. 'Yes, actually it's the perfect place for some illicit romancing, isn't it? Tucked away in the deep, dark woods!'

'Better warn them about the spiders and scorpions and snakes and bats,' Pankaj said, 'or they might just freak out.'

'I think those would make it even more exciting,' Anshu said wickedly.

Khushboo was quite excited by Anshu's suggestion. I listened on the extension:

Besides, if anyone had noticed, they'd have been down here by now.'

'So you think we should bring them down here after they get married?' Lavina asked.

Anshu nodded. 'Yes, just as long as they're in danger from Vineet and Biker…'

'Knowing them, that'll be forever,' I said as Anshu glared at me. She put her hands on her hips: oh, oh, lecture coming!

'I just don't get it! Just because they have different religions they can't like or love each other. All religions say that human beings must be loving and kind, generous and selfless and giving and…so what is the *goddamn problem?* If all religions preach that we should love one another, then all religions should encourage people to fall in love because that's when people love each other the most and are most happy. Instead they try and do the opposite: you can't hold hands, kissing is forbidden, you can't sit next to each other or hug each other, forget about anything else. But oh yes, it's perfectly fine (and a ticket to heaven) if you cut off people's heads or lynch them and hate them in the name of religion! Bah! What they really should be doing is to make people stay in love with each other forever. That's what all the priests and swamijis and maulvis and whatevers should be preaching. Even better they should *encourage* people of *different* religions to fall in love and marry one another—not forbid it! If I were PM I'd give *incentives* to people to do that—what Lav's parents have done! Instead these stupid politicians just try to make people hate each other by pitting one religion against another and organizing lynch mobs. Have you watched the crap they dish out on TV? It makes me sick to the stomach! And they're all much the same—the whole sordid bunch of them!'

Wow! We all stared at Anshu open-mouthed.

'Adults..,' Shiv said mournfully as Anshu, red with emotion, sat down beside him, 'are the biggest sanctimonious hypocrites in the entire universe.' Quietly he put his arm around her.

'Yes,' Pankaj added, 'they're always lecturing us on how to behave and then there's Parliament! Have you seen what goes on there? If we behaved that way in class…' He made a dramatic throat-cutting gesture.

Nasreen's eyes glittered suddenly. 'And have you noticed how nearly all the wars in the world have been started by men?'

Shiv, Pankaj and I exchanged glances.

'Yes,' Pankaj shot back, 'but you know spider women eat spider men and so does the lady praying mantis and…it's nearly always the girls who choose which guys they want to go around with, which is what makes the guys fight each other and start wars…'

Nasreen lunged at him and gave him a huge unexpected hug. His spectacles nearly fell off. 'I'll eat you in one gulp, spider man, if you're not careful!' she said huskily, making him go scarlet.

I glanced at Lavina. I would certainly go to war for her! She caught my glance and guessed what I had thought because she smiled sweetly at me.

'So you think we ought to bring Khushboo and Salim here?' Shiv asked. Anshu nodded.

'I think it might be a good idea. If everything is all right then there'll be no need for them to come here, but if there's trouble this will be the perfect bolt-hole! Actually, I think we ought to show them this place ASAP.' She looked at all of us, one by one. 'I know it will mean giving up our own hideout—but we're not hiding from anyone. They might have to!'

'We could bring them here once we know for sure that they need a place to hide,' I said. 'No need to show them before that.'

All the girls shook their heads at once. 'No,' Anshu said, 'they need to know as soon as possible and much before any balloon goes up. Suppose we're not around, say at school, and something happens and they have to run? We have to show them this place at the earliest, I think.'

Well, there went our hideout! But I knew that Anshu was right. For us this was just an exciting place to hang out in (with an infuriating mystery attached), but for Khushboo and Salim it could be a proper sanctuary. And then suddenly it struck me like a blow to the solar plexus: Khushboo and Salim would *have* to get married—or elope—before 2nd May. They would absolutely need a place to hide out in before that.

'So when do we tell them and bring them here?'

'We'll tell them as soon as we get home and bring them here tomorrow,' Anshu said decisively. 'Tomorrow's Saturday. We could combine it with our trip to Malcha Mahal. We could go there first and then come here and make it a day's outing.'

We all nodded.

Then Lavina looked around. 'I think we ought to tidy up this place before we leave. We can't show them a pigsty!'

We grinned. 'Yeah, just what will they think of us?' Anshu chuckled.

But the next day there were all kinds of hiccups awaiting our grand plan. First Pankaj and then Shiv both rang up to say they wouldn't be able to make it—their families were demanding their presence. Pankaj was being dragged off to a relative's farmhouse for the day and Shiv had to go shopping with his parents, 'which with Mom and Dad means pretty much the whole day on the road'. Then Mom said that Anshu had a major (read: possible root canal) dentist's appointment at around midday and we knew that would take at least three hours. So Nasreen decided that she'd go to see some other friends of hers, who lived in Gurgaon. But all that didn't really count (well, in a way it did, in a very big way) because Khushboo couldn't make it either. She said, disturbingly, that Biker's parents had been invited over to sort out details related to the wedding and she had to remain home all day.

'Then are you free on Sunday?' Anshu asked Khushboo on the phone. 'If so, block it! We'd like you to take us to Malcha Mahal on a historical tour. And then…and then we'd like to take you and Salim Bhai to another very special place, which I think you'd like!' She grinned mischievously down the phone and winked at me.

'No, I'm not going to tell you where: it'll be a surprise!' she told Khushboo. 'But it's somewhere you can be safe from Vineet and Biker. You know, you'll have to either get married or run away before the 2nd of May.'

Then she frowned as she listened to what Khushboo was telling her. Quickly, I picked up the extension line and eavesdropped:

'Anshu, actually Salim and I have already made plans to escape. We have our tickets and all our documents ready. We're not going to tell you guys when or where we will be going and if we'll return: the less you know the better…'

Both Anshu and I immediately saw the problem with this.

'But we have to tell Vineet every time we take you for an outing. He won't allow you out otherwise. We pick you up and drop you back personally. So how will you leave the house?'

'I'll just tell him that I'm meeting you all at the site; you know, I think ever since that zoo expedition, he's sort of lowered his guard and has actually been nice to me, even offering to take me sari shopping, can you imagine! I think he'll let me go on my own…' She paused. 'And then…when the balloon goes up, you can truthfully say that there never was a trip planned at that time: that I had pulled the wool over everyone's eyes. He'll be hopping mad of course, but at me, not at you guys.'

Again, we were not convinced.

'Didi, just in case he refuses to let you go alone, you call us,' my indefatigable sister said. 'Then you disappear with Salim Bhai and we'll run back home hysterically screaming that you gave us the slip. That we searched everywhere but couldn't find you.'

'Dear, I don't think Vineet will buy that.'

'Maybe you could write a letter to your family

saying that we are not to blame, that we had no idea you were hatching this plan all along,' Anshu went on.

'Yes!' I piped in, 'after all we are just dumb kids who needed tuition in nearly every subject!'

'Umi! You are very sweet! Let me discuss this with Salim the next time we meet.'

'That'll be on Sunday, Didi,' Anshu reminded her.

Suddenly I was assailed by another doubt. Really, was I the only thinking person in this gang? I put down the extension and went up to Anshu to whisper in her ear.

'Anshu, how will we take them there? Do you think Salim's Scooty will be able to bash through those narrow paths from Malcha Mahal to the step-well? It's tough enough getting our cycles through. And we'd never get it through the gully to the moat.'

'Oh!' she frowned, putting her hand over the phone. 'Good you thought about that now, Umi, and we didn't realize it too late. We'll ask them to hire bicycles. Khushboo can say this is a bicycle tour she's taking us on considering we're so mad about bikes.' She uncovered the receiver: 'Listen, Khushboo Didi, we'll make this a cycle tour. You and Salim Bhai can hire bikes from Lulu Cycles in the market here—he's the fellow who looks after ours. Okay then, you speak to Salim Bhai and get back to me. Bye, Didi!'

'Great,' she said and smiled. 'That's done. Now

come on let's go down and feed the dogs. They must be waiting!'

They were. All our families took turns feeding them, and today was our turn. We went down with the packets of dog food and found them all sitting in front of their bowls, waiting impatiently. Nasreen had really trained them well!

'Well guys,' I told them, 'tomorrow it's just going to be you guys and me, messing about here all day.'

That's when the idea began to unravel in my brain; it would require some bold planning on my part but… but if it worked…

So, just a little later when Anshu went in for her bath and the coast was clear, I picked up the phone, dialled and took a very deep breath indeed…

But dammit, dammit, dammit! At dinner, Anshu kept glancing my way and raising her eyebrows quizzically and winking.

'What?' I asked, irritated. 'What's the problem?'

'Nothing,' she smirked and shrugged and took a bite of her chicken. 'Ma, this chicken is really good!'

'Thank you, dear!'

Afterwards, while we watched TV, she kept on glancing my way and gently whacked the back of my head a couple of times.

'Why did you do that? What's your problem?'

'No problem, Umi! Should there be one?'

'I don't know what you're talking about!'

She winked big time. 'I think you do!'

As we prepared for bed she came and sat at the edge of mine.

'What do you want?' I asked her truculently. She grinned.

'I know you've fixed up to go with Lavina to the den tomorrow,' she said. 'And judging by your face she's probably agreed: you're looking like the cat that's taken the cream. You've been beaming all evening and I've seen how you are when she's around. She has a soft spot for you even if she may be a little old for you.'

Dammit, dammit, dammit!

'So...so what's the big deal?' I asked hotly. 'It's a good place to hang out in!'

'Sure,' she said, grinning. Suddenly she sobered down. 'Umi, just one thing: take the dogs with you. Don't go there alone, okay? Promise me that or I'll tell Ma that you too have a toothache and she'll drag you to the dentist too.'

'Of course I'll take the dogs!' I said. 'We never go to the Ridge without them.'

'Good! Then you guys have a good time.' She gave me a peck on the cheek. I told you: my elder sister was a bit weird.

'So how's your er...thing with Shiv getting along?'

I asked, determined to get a bit of my own back. She grinned.

'He's a goofy softball or a softy goofball, I really don't know which.'

I grinned. 'So you and he…so you and he are…?'

'Huh? What?' she barked. 'Now mind your own business and go to sleep, you little pipsqueak!' She strode out of the room, switching off the light.

Tomorrow was going to be a beautiful day.

9

Mom nearly sabotaged my elaborate plan the next morning, but quick thinking on my part saved the day. At breakfast she looked at me and smiled.

'Beta, I have to take your sister to the dentist this afternoon. Maybe you should come along—I don't like leaving you home alone.'

Anshu gave me a sympathetic look and then ruined it all by grinning maliciously.

'Yeah, he might put eggs in the microwave again.'

'Mom…umm…I have cricket coaching with Salim Bhai this afternoon,' I bluffed frantically. Thankfully she swallowed it hook, line and sinker.

'In that case it's okay. We should be back by around 4 or 4.30. And I'll ring up to check if all is well.' She smiled fondly at me.

'Mom, but I won't be home and you don't allow us to have mobiles.'

'Yes,' Anshu joined in, 'if you let us have mobiles,

you would never have to worry where we are and could be a proper helicopter parent!'

'What? Hmm…well we'll see about that. I'll have a word with your father.'

'Great!'

I quickly called Salim. 'Sir, if my mom calls or you meet her and she talks to you please tell her that you'll be coaching us this afternoon…'

'What?'

'Please, sir!'

He was smart and caught on quickly. 'Okay, no problem, don't worry! After all you guys have done for us this is the least I could do.'

'Thank you, sir!'

Shiv thankfully was already out of the way.

I was like a cat on a hot tin roof all morning looking at my watch every fifteen minutes. It promised to be a really great day: it had clouded over and cooled down and the forecast had predicted a 'thunderstorm with squalls' for the late evening. At last Anshu and Mom left.

'Bye!' I said to my sister. 'Be good. Don't bite the dentist!'

She glared at me; I could see the poor thing was nervous. Who wouldn't be?

At last the coast was clear. At 2 p.m. after having eaten my lunch and cleaned the plates (which, I had been told to do) I rang Lavina.

'Hi, are you ready?'

'Hey, Umi, yeah. I'll meet you in the park in about twenty minutes, okay?'

'Sure! I'll round up the dogs in the meanwhile.'

And then we were actually off! Just the two of us and the Six Pack, delighted to be on the move again and clearing the path ahead for us.

'We're like those VIPs,' I yelled happily at Lavina, 'With our pilots clearing the way ahead.'

She smiled and nodded as we sailed on.

I had put on my newest jeans and a smart grey and black T-shirt and had debated on whether to splash on a little of one of my father's fancy colognes. But colognes are big tell-tales, and Ma's nose is razor sharp. Plus Anshu would just tease me to death about it and there'd be endless questions, so I decided not to. Besides they always said that girls are more attracted to a guy's natural, manly smell.

Lavina was in frayed denim shorts and a sleeveless white top held up with very thin straps with bows on the shoulders. She had a denim jacket on top of that which she removed as soon as we entered the Ridge. Her hair shone like a forest fire and I told her so.

'Go on,' she said good-naturedly.

'You've brought your swimsuit?' I asked, pointing to her blue knapsack.

'Swimsuit, towel, hard-boiled eggs, chaklis, scones and chocolate.'

'Great!'

We trundled off side by side down the horse-riding trail with the dogs running easily beside us. At first it was kind of prickly and hot and very still, and we had begun perspiring. I had begun wondering if it was going to be a really stifling afternoon. But suddenly there were delicious drafts of cool, moist breeze that made the trees rustle and sway.

'Lovely!' Lavina said—and that's what I thought she was too—but kept my mouth shut this time.

'Yeah, they said there might be a thunderstorm in the evening.'

Suddenly I felt really good, almost buoyant.

'Are you feeling upbeat?' I asked Lavina. She nodded and then grinned at me.

'Yes, I am.'

'That's probably because the air is charged with negative ions. They say they make you feel good.'

'Oh,' she said and made a duckface.

'And of course because I'm with you,' I quickly added, 'that's why I'm feeling good!'

'Dufus! I know.' She sniffed the air appreciatively. 'Smells like wet earth. I just love the smell, it's so rich and fragrant. It must be raining somewhere close by.'

She'd barely said that when it suddenly became really dark like it was late in the evening.

'Looks like it's going to rain very soon!' she went on, sitting up straight, turning her face upwards.

Ahead we could barely pick out the trail in the gloom. We switched on our bike lights.

'We're well sheltered under these trees,' I said.

There came a sudden blinding flash and an ear-splitting explosion, followed by a drum-roll of thunder. Lightning had struck not very far away! Peacocks called stridently from all over the place in a paroxysm of joy.

'Oh my god, the storm's going to hit!' Lavina yelled, as the dogs looked startled and turned to us for reassurance. Then I became aware of the roar—in the distance first—the sort of sound waves make on the surf, but getting closer and louder by the second. And suddenly twisters of dust were rising from the forest floor along with millions of dead leaves that were doing frenetic dervish-like dances. Gusts of wind buffeted us. The trees bent and swayed.

'It's here!' Lavina yelled as her bike wobbled erratically. 'Yikes, this wind is getting a bit crazy.'

I knew it wasn't safe to be in a forest during a thunderstorm—not so much because of the lightning as because of the deadwood that might fall, not to mention entire trees. But we'd come well over halfway and it would take longer to go back than ahead. The dogs were looking at us, obviously awaiting instructions.

'Yeah, let's just speed up a bit if we can!' I yelled. 'We're nearly at the turn-off now.'

She just nodded. 'I guess. But I don't like being in the middle of these things,' she said. 'They make me nervous.'

'Heck, do you hear that? That's not rain!' I yelled. The roaring wind was now accompanied by a solid pitter patter as if handfuls of pebbles were falling.

'Look! It's hail!' Lavina said, pointing at small white pebble-like things bouncing down through the canopy and on to the path.

We just focused now on riding as fast as we could, our heads down. The rain, which had become quite heavy, was being pummelled every which way by the wind, even coming at us horizontally, though fortunately most of the hailstones that hit us had been deflected by foliage before landing on our heads and shoulders. But what was really scary were the dead branches that kept cracking and tumbling down, sometimes pretty large ones judging by the loud crashing sound they made as they thudded to earth, bringing down a welter of small branches, twigs and leaves with them. One of them could easily take us out. At last we arrived at the turn-off to the narrow trail: we'd have to ride single file from here on and push our cycles through sections. The dogs stayed close to us.

I led the way, ducking my head under the low branches and looking back every now and then. Lavina pushed her bicycle along and smiled.

'It's getting pretty scary,' she panted, pushing her wet hair out of her face, rain streaming down it. By now we were both soaked through. 'The sooner we get to the step-well the better.'

'Yeah!' I winced as a huge branch crashed somewhere to the left of us. 'I don't like this!'

We'd just manoeuvred past a swaying, creaking old neem tree when we heard an ominous CRACK! right above us. A bough from the tree as thick as a Metro pillar thudded down just behind us making the dogs yelp with fright and scuttle ahead. The ground shook as if it was a small earthquake tremor.

'Oh my god!' Lavina screamed, her face white. She was trembling. Ashen-faced myself, I stared at the huge fractured bough lying across the path: if we had come by just seconds later, we would have been pulp. Then Dada whined. I looked around for him. He and the others had gathered under a low rocky overhang just adjacent to the path. They crouched inside and looked at us, their tails wagging. I grabbed Lavina's hand.

'Come on, we'll shelter here till this lunatic storm passes.'

We dropped our bikes and crawled inside. Very sweetly the dogs made room for us and we all huddled under the overhang, peering out as twigs and branches tumbled through the canopy and the hailstones bounced about crazily. Sitting next to me, Lavina suddenly turned and put her arms around me and rested her face against my chest. She was still trembling, and I think so was I.

'That branch,' she said in a small voice, 'if we had passed by five seconds earlier...' She clutched me tightly.

'We should be safe here,' I said, hardly believing that I was actually (heroically) reassuring and comforting my girlfriend in a shallow cave on the Delhi Ridge. 'But look, that little path has already become a rivulet! It must be really coming down.'

'That was too close,' Lavina whispered again. 'We could have been...'

'Don't think about it,' I said, now in superman mode. 'Thank god Dada alerted us to this place.'

We looked at the dogs. Bedraggled and miserable they huddled together but their eyes were calm, they knew they were safe and that we just had to wait out the storm.

'Storms like this are really scary,' Lavina said in a tearful voice. 'I don't like them one bit! It's like...like Mother Nature is out to get you.'

'I know what you mean. But we're safe here now.' She rested her head against my chest again making me feel even more heroic.

'You know, your heart is beating really fast,' she said, looking up at me with a small smile. 'I can feel it thumping away. It sounds like a galloping racehorse.'

I hoped she had guessed the reason why.

'Adrenaline's probably pumping.'

We were still hit by occasional gusts of wind and rain, which made us gasp, but at least there was no danger from falling trees or branches.

'Oh,' Lavina suddenly squealed, looking down at herself. 'My top is virtually transparent now. It's like wet tissue paper!'

'Oh? I hadn't noticed,' I lied. She looked up at me again and smiled.

'You're such a bad liar, and such a cute dufus,' she chided me gently: And then planted her lips on mine and gave me this really long, lingering kiss.

Now I knew for sure that she was my girlfriend and she knew why my heart had sounded like a galloping racehorse.

But then Badi-Dadi whined and wriggling over the others thrust her wet nose between our faces and licked Lavina's nose.

'Ugh! Badi-Dadi you've got such bad breath,' Lavina squealed and jerked back. She smiled, her brown eyes shining as she re-tied the bows of her top, which had come undone. I must have turned to complete goo as I stared at her mesmerized. Lady Bouncer had now joined Badi-Dadi and was giving my face a workout; her whole bottom wagging.

'Ugh, you guys…get back!'

But would they back off? Now they wanted to climb into our laps! And wet dogs don't exactly smell nice. But there was nothing we could do but exchange sheepish looks and comfort the dogs in our laps.

'Look, the storm seems to be passing,' Lavina said after about fifteen minutes. The surf-like roar had lessened considerably and now the main sound was the steady plink-plonk of raindrops falling from the foliage. The wind had suddenly dropped.

'That was quite a temper tantrum from Mother Nature, wasn't it?' Lavina said, taking my hand as we began to crawl out together. 'We were nearly done for!'

'Yeah, I wonder how many trees it's brought down in town.'

We picked up our bikes and began making our way through the battered forest again. After our first foray from Malcha Mahal to the step-well, we had always carried a large kitchen knife (in lieu of a machete) with us and had used this very effectively to clear the way where necessary. Now, we really had to hack our way through sections where thorny branches and twigs lay

door of the den. I looked at the dogs wondering if they would go stir-crazy again. They did sniff around excitedly everywhere but none of them did anything crazy this time.

'Every time we come here I wonder whose place this is,' I told Lavina as I sat down on the huge bed. She'd switched on the rod heater and arrayed our wet clothes in front of it on a very fancy wooden rack, facing one wall.

'Bless them, whoever they are,' she said. 'Now let's have something to eat.'

I shook my head. 'You know, I keep getting the feeling that I've forgotten to do something vital,' I went on. 'It struck me the very first time we came here, but I've just forgotten what it was.'

'Don't worry, it'll come back when it needs to,' she said and sat beside me.

'And I keep thinking how does anyone get here except via the tunnel? It just doesn't make sense!'

'Umi, you worry too much.'

'Someone in the gang has to,' I said dolefully. She put her arms around me and hugged me.

'I guess,' she said, looking at me searchingly.

'Whuff! Woof! Woof!'

'Badi-Dadi, what the...?' Lavina squealed as the damn dog suddenly tried to get into her lap, barking indignantly. The others were sitting around us and now each one of them began barking, their tails wagging in a blur. Lavina put her hands in front of her face.

'Oh my god, I don't believe it! These dogs are stopping us from making out!'

'They must be jealous. Hey stop it you guys, mind your own business.'

But would they? Not a chance. The maximum they permitted was for us to hold hands. Anything more and they were all over our case. They'd use their most irritating barks too, the shrill, indignant ones that could make glass bowls ping.

'I'll bet our parents are behind this. They must have secretly trained them to behave like this,' I said darkly. 'That's why they don't worry when we take them along with us.'

Lavina giggled. 'You guys are really such a bunch of killjoy nannies,' she scolded them, but patted them on the heads at the same time. 'You should join the government.'

'Yeah,' I said sourly. I looked at the pack in disgust and then at Lavina. Who knows to what giddy heights our budding romance would have reached if not for these interfering busybody pooches?

Still, we had a pretty good time in each other's company. It felt so good just to be in the same room as her and knowing that she felt the same way about me. We ate our boiled eggs and chaklis and scones and chocolates and chatted. But we couldn't even sit on the sofa together side by side, without having one of the dogs (Badi-Dadi was the queen bee here) trying to get between us or on our laps or barking into our faces. We had to sit on separate chairs, and they would sit around our feet and grin up at us with their tails thumping on the floor as though they'd accomplished something great. It was ridiculous.

'I wonder what Khushboo and Salim will think of this place,' I said.

'We'll know when we bring them over tomorrow. They should like it.'

'Whew, it's beginning to get hot in here now,' I said after a while. 'Our clothes must be dry by now. Maybe we should turn off the heater.'

The clothes were still slightly damp but not clammy or anything. We changed turn by turn in the bathroom with no mishap this time and grinned sheepishly at each other.

'Now maybe we should think about getting back,' Lavina glanced at her watch. 'God knows how much havoc the storm has created on the paths. We might have to take a diversion or something.'

God knows when I'd be alone with her without the dogs again.

'They really are a Nanny Pack!' I said glowering at the happy dogs.

There were innumerable branches and twigs strewn all over the paths on the way back and we had quite a time manoeuvring our bicycles over or around them. We were lucky (again) with the big bough that had nearly flattened us. It was a huge curved and forked branch, and was lying on the ground in such a way that there was a gap under which we could crawl, dragging our bicycles behind us. The dogs just slunk under it easily. We eyed our overhang shelter again. Well at least we'd been able to canoodle a bit there! For me it would always be a special place.

Poor Anshu was looking like she'd done ten rounds with Mike Tyson when she got back from the dentist. First he had made them wait for hours and then they had got caught in traffic jams on the way back. That didn't deter her from cross-examining me though.

'How was the date?' she mumbled as if her mouth was full of mashed potato, but still grinning. And added: 'Don't worry: I'll be cross-checking whatever you tell me with Lav. Did you get caught in the storm?'

'Yes, but we found shelter...A huge branch nearly fell on us. We could have been killed.' That didn't seem to bother my loving elder sister one bit.

'Did you...?' she asked me archly instead, and looked at me knowingly, raising her eyebrows.

'Did we what? No, we didn't swim. We'd got soaked before that!'

'I didn't mean swim. I meant…you know what I meant!' She winked and made awful kissing sounds

'Anshu, you have to be clear. Did we what?'

'Ooo, so you did!'

'We didn't! Those damn dogs…' I blurted.

'What?' she said cocking her head: 'The dogs?'

'Better ask them,' I said sourly. 'Nasreen seems to have trained them in a convent or something.'

Anshu was giggling as she picked up the phone and dialled Lavina to ask her what I was talking about. She didn't stop giggling after Lavina told her what happened with those wretched dogs.

'Woo-woo!' she hooted, pinching my cheeks, 'woo-woo!'

But then she got down to fixing tomorrow's great 'tryst' between Khushboo and Salim.

'We will get to the Mahal by 3 or 3.15,' Anshu said, her eyes gleaming. 'We can leave them to romance for about an hour, say till 4 o'clock. And we could be at the den by 4.30 or so and show them the place. Leave by around 5.30 and be back home like good children a little after 6 p.m. Perfect!'

10

It was early next morning that I suddenly remembered what I'd forgotten to do regarding our secret den; something I ought to have done right at the beginning to try and pinpoint its exact location. Anshu had said we might be under Connaught Place and I think Lavina had mentioned we might even pop out under Parliament House. I knew we had followed a fairly consistent north-eastern direction after we left Malcha Mahal that first morning and had ridden for 1.2 km. The tunnel had gone due east from here, leading to the secret shelter, which was a further 750 metres away. This was enough to go on.

I switched on the desktop and got onto Google Earth. I printed out a map of the Ridge that showed Malcha Mahal and the section of the Ridge north-east of it. On this I drew out the north-eastern quadrant and drew a circle with the radius equivalent of 1.2 km using Malcha Mahal as the centre. We'd gone nearly directly north-east all the way, so I drew a series of straight lines radiating either way from, and through, dead north-east to the circumference of my circle from Malcha Mahal. Hah! Now I had several possible locations of the step-well. Even if it was roughly accurate it would do. I drew circles with a radius equivalent of 750 metres, using the step-well locations as the centre, and from each of them took a line due east and pinned the locations where they each intersected the circumference of the circles.

And man, was I blown away! I couldn't believe my eyes when I saw what one of the intercepts was showing! Suddenly everything—well nearly everything—began making a whole lot of sense.

I knocked perfunctorily on Anshu's bedroom door and barged in, the map in my hand. She was still fast asleep.

'Anshu wake up, I figured out where our bomb-shelter den is,' I yelled, shaking her.

'Urghhmph! What the heck! Umi I'm going to hit you! Do you know the time? Get the hell out of my room!'

'I said I know where the secret bomb-shelter is. You won't believe it. Wake up!'

I stood back. Anshu could be like a cobra when woken up like this, so it was better to keep one's distance. Sure enough she reared up and swung a pillow at me.

'Grrumph, if you don't get out of my room this instant, I won't be responsible!'

'Anshu, I found the location of the secret bomb-shelter. It all fits in!'

'I don't care. The room is not going to run away. But you'd better if you know what's good for you.'

She turned on her side and covered her head with her pillow and growled some more.

Girls!

❧

The whole gang turned up for lunch later that day, excited by the afternoon's prospects. With great pride I showed them the findings on my map. Well, they seemed more excited about how Khushboo and Salim would react to the secret bomb-shelter, than about where it was. Pankaj was the only one who seemed a bit impressed and interested.

'Great,' he said, but then frowned, 'but it still doesn't explain why there's no door in the shelter leading up to the place. We've searched and searched and found squat.'

I shrugged. 'Maybe they thought they wouldn't need the room any more and just sealed it up. There may have been a trapdoor in the ceiling or something, which they cemented up or sealed with those stones.'

'But why cover up all the furniture and leave all the tins there to rust? And why is the tunnel entrance still open then? They ought to have sealed that up too.'

'God knows! You know how these people think! Mostly they don't seem to be able to.' I rolled my eyes.

'Hey guys,' Lavina came up to us, her eyes shining. 'Guess what? It's Khushboo's birthday tomorrow. See what we've got her.'

'And yes, since it is from all of us you guys need to cough up Rs 250 each,' Nasreen smirked.

They'd bought Khushboo a dark-blue and gold handbag, if you please. 'See…' Lavina said, grinning, 'it even has a secret compartment for a mobile phone.'

'You spent, what three thousand rupees on a *handbag*?'

'That's not all that much, you moron! Now pay!'

'Hmph!' But I was still thinking about the mystery surrounding the bomb-shelter. If it had been deliberately sealed, then the tunnel would have been sealed up too. So, if it had not been sealed, and had just been forgotten in the course of time there ought to still be an entrance—which we had not found and by god, we had searched high and low for it. We had come up with nothing.

Our departure for Malcha Mahal got delayed to about 5.30 p.m., because Khushboo couldn't manage to get away earlier, but it really didn't matter. With the dogs and two adults accompanying us we were quite okay even if we were out till 7-7.30 p.m.

'What have you told Vineet?' Anshu asked Khushboo with a grin. 'Where are you taking us today? On a cycle tour?'

'Oh,' she replied smiling, 'I told him we'd be biking along New Delhi's beautiful tree-lined avenues. I wanted to show you the different trees that were planted along them. You know, along Akbar Road, and APJ Kalam Marg, and Amrita Shergill Marg, and Lodi Road and so on. And to show you how the Brits planned the whole Central Vista and North and South Blocks...' She shook her head. 'It doesn't really matter. Vineet just nodded and I heard him fix a bike ride with Biker and his friends along the Yamuna beyond Kalindi Kunj. So he'll be safely out of our way.'

'Cool! Maybe after that zoo expedition he's decided to trust you and not follow you anymore,' Anshu grinned.

We whizzed down Sardar Patel Road (with the Six Pack) and turned into Bistadari Road where Salim was waiting for us with his hired bike. And finally we were at Malcha Mahal again, thankfully deserted once more.

'Ta-da! Here we are!' sang Anshu like she was a fairy-godmother or something. 'How does it feel to be back here after so long, Khushboo Didi?' she grinned cheekily.

Khushboo just went pink as she glanced at Salim who grinned a bit sheepishly.

'You guys just chill here for a bit, we're going for a quick spin with the dogs,' Anshu went on, winking meaningfully at Lavina and me. 'We'll be back in about half an hour or so.'

We rattled off along the trail leading to the step-well, leaving Khushboo and Salim at the entrance, holding hands and waving to us and smiling.

'Okay guys, we give them half an hour at least, so we turn back in about twenty minutes,' Anshu said, standing on her pedals and accelerating. The trail was strewn with twigs and branches brought down by the storm no doubt, which we cleared away. Now when we brought Khushboo and Salim down this trail on their regular road bikes they'd have a smoother ride. At one point a huge creeper-like vine lay right across the path like the tangle of cables you normally see in Chandni Chowk. This was about halfway down the slope that led to the large pool into which Anshu had tumbled on our first visit. We shifted the lianas and vines to the side of the trail: some of them were really tough and thorny and could cut into your hands if you pulled at them carelessly or too hard. It took us ten or fifteen minutes to clear the trail properly. After that, we decided to go back to the Mahal.

'We're going to have to wade through the pool

again,' Shiv said, glancing at it. 'Wonder if Khushboo and Salim will be willing to do that.'

'Bet they will,' Anshu said. 'Besides they can always wash their feet in the well later on.'

We had just about reached Malcha Mahal when the dogs suddenly stiffened up again like they had done when we had first come here. They'd been leading but now they slowed down and stopped, their ears pricked, fur beginning to bristle. The hair rose along the backs of their necks and they got all stiff-legged and stiff-tailed.

'What the…?' Nasreen looked at them and signalled us to stop. 'What is it, guys?' She ushered us to keep quiet and dismount and approach with care. Suddenly I got a very bad feeling in the pit of my stomach.

'There's someone else at the Mahal,' Nasreen whispered, holding Dada by the collar. 'Easy, boy!'

'Should we call out?'

Nasreen shook her head. 'Let's see who it is first.'

Hah, I suddenly thought, glancing at Lavina. Maybe it was just Khushboo and Salim having a nice kiss and the dogs were doing their Nanny Pack act all over again.

But then we froze. We heard the dull sickening thwack of something heavy hitting flesh and bone, a grunt of pain, and a shriek.

'Oh my god!' Anshu and Lavina whispered, both of them going pale

Keeping low, commando style, we crawled along the path, our eyes peeled as the gaunt monument ahead slowly came into view. There were four dirt bikes parked in front of it. Coming down the steps were Vineet, Biker and two other hoodlum types. Vineet had a cricket bat in his hand—a bat I recognized: it was Raghav's! But between Vineet and Biker and his friends were Khushboo, her churidar-suit half ripped away, her hair a mess, and Salim, shirtless. Their hands were bound behind their backs, their faces red: raw, bloody and pulpy. They'd been badly beaten and hardly seemed to know what was happening.

'Vineet, what are you going to do? Let us be! Are you mad?' Khushboo gasped. Vineet said nothing but put a ham-like hand around her throat and began to squeeze it. Then he snatched her dupatta, tore a strip and gagged his sister.

Biker clouted Salim over the head with a steel knuckleduster. Salim gasped, his eyes bulging as another punch landed in the stomach.

Beside me, I could feel Nasreen stiffen. She was holding on to Dada and the rest of the pack was bristling behind him, growling, low and deep down in their throats.

Khushboo shook her head desperately, her eyes beginning to bulge. Vineet punched her low in the stomach and she keeled over coughing. The other hoodlum pulled her upright by her hair. Then Vineet nodded at Biker and the other two.

We watched, frozen with horror, as Vineet and one of the hoodlums dragged Salim away and Biker took hold of Khushboo. Suddenly Lavina clutched me and pointed, her face completely white. On a nearby thick horizontal branch two ropes dangled with nooses at their ends. Vineet and his friend were dragging Salim to one of them and then forced him up on a tall stool they'd dragged out. Then they slipped the noose over his head. Biker and the other fellow held Khushboo by her hair, forcing her to watch, even as she tried to struggle.

I glanced sideways at the others all lying down flat on the ground. Pankaj had his camera glued to his eye. He had been filming the whole scene, right from the start, though I could see his hands were trembling. Shiv looked appalled and kept glancing at Anshu, awaiting orders no doubt. Anshu was prodding Nasreen and glaring at her. Lavina looked like she was about to faint.

Vineet looked at Biker and nodded impatiently, and made an obscene gesture with the cricket bat. Biker grinned. His fingers gripped the top of Khushboo's churidar suit and he leered right into her face.

That was enough for Nasreen.

'Go get them boys!' she yelled, releasing Dada, 'Take them down!'

Snarling and barking ferociously the pack obeyed: all of them knew both Khushboo and Salim as friends, so instinctively went for the goons. Dada took Biker down, and Badi-Dadi launched herself at Vineet. The others divided the two hoodlums between them. The men screamed and scrambled to their feet, fending off the dogs the best they could and fled desperately back up into the monument, yelling with fright, chased by the pack. Shiv, Anshu, Lavina, Pankaj and I raced up to a stunned Khushboo and Salim and cut them loose, while Nasreen watched the dogs, gleefully egging them on.

'Come on, let's go!' Anshu yelled. 'On your bikes, everyone!' Then she looked at Khushboo and Salim. 'Can you ride?' she asked desperately. They just nodded dumbly.

'Let's go, let's go! Nasreen, come on now!'

The snarling, barking and shouting continued for several moments, enabling us to vanish down the trail. But then: a sound that chilled us. Two shots rang out, echoing around the monument, followed by the shrill yelping of a dog—and the clapping of wings as pigeons blustered out of the monument. Nasreen put her fingers in her mouth and whistled. The Six Pack streamed out of Malcha Mahal. Only now there were just five of them. They raced after us.

'Come on guys, let's go,' Nasreen yelled as the pack joined us. 'Lady-B, no! Come here, girl!'

'Oh god, they got Badmash,' I said. 'He's not with them.'

Already a fair distance ahead, Anshu followed by Khushboo and Salim, was pedalling away as hard as she could. Shiv followed them with Pankaj and Lavina behind him. For a change I had Nasreen with me bringing up the rear. The dogs were now with us.

'Hope those guys are down for a bit,' I gasped at Nasreen as we pedalled frantically. She nodded. 'Poor Badmash, they got him,' she said. 'Hope they've been bitten good and proper.' But then she looked back and turned ashen.

The raucous snarling of dirt bikes starting up reached us, following by a roaring of the engines.

'Those bikes will be able to ride down this trail easily and catch up with us.'

'Just pedal Umi, pedal,' Nasreen panted.

But within minutes it was clear that the bikes would catch up very quickly indeed.

'Should I set the dogs on them again?' Nasreen asked, glancing at me. I shook my head.

'They've got guns. They'll take them down like sitting ducks. We've already lost Badmash.'

She nodded. Ahead the others were strung out: Anshu well in the lead. I don't know how Khushboo and Salim managed to keep up with her considering the state they were in; I guess terror lends you wings.

Shiv and Pankaj followed them closely and Lavina had slowed down a bit, looking back towards me and Nasreen. Behind us we could hear the dirt bikes get louder. Our only advantage was that the bikes would have to travel single file and hopefully none of the riders had ridden down this trail before, so they wouldn't be familiar with the terrain.

We reached the slope leading to the pool in record time and I heard Anshu yell out a warning to everyone as she splashed into it. I was just beginning down the slope when I had my idea and slammed on my brakes, skidding to a halt. Nasreen glanced back at me and yelled.

'Umi, what the heck are you doing? Come on now, you moron!'

She stopped and Lavina crammed on her brakes and stopped too.

I raced to the side of the trail where we had dumped all the tangled-up lianas and vines that we had so recently moved and began stringing them across the path again, tying them around the trunk of trees on the other side. Nasreen caught on immediately and joined me to help.

'Wind them around any tree trunk,' I gasped. 'Tie them as tightly as you can.'

Lavina had dropped her cycle and come running up to us. 'I'll keep watch,' she yelled. 'You focus on the job.'

'Thanks!'

The dirt bikes were getting closer by the second. Any moment they'd breast the rise.

The engines' roar rose to a crescendo and then there they were, rearing up in a brief wheelie before crashing back down on both wheels, two orange bikes side by side, in spite of the narrow trail, coming at us insanely fast. Biker and Vineet both had pistols in their hands and were clutching on to the handlebars and half-standing up, looking murderous. They saw us and raised their guns and fired, just as we turned to flee. Nasreen squealed and I suddenly felt I'd been heftily punched and slashed and then stung in the bottom by a red-hot hornet. I jerked forward, staggered and nearly fell.

'Yikes!' I yelped, jumping up. Miraculously the burning sensation just vanished, but I knew I'd been hit.

'Go Umi, go!' Lavina screamed. 'Get on your bike! They're shooting!' Nasreen was standing stock still staring blankly at her arm down which blood was pouring. Then she was galvanized into action and got on her bike as I did. I found that I couldn't sit in the saddle—the red-hot sting was still there! So I just stood up and pedalled. Lavina brought up the rear now and ushered us along like a hysterical sheepdog. What a girl! She would take any more bullets that followed squarely in her back!

Within seconds Vineet and Biker hit the lianas we had strung across the trail. Together they were strong enough to send the bikes toppling high and landing halfway down the slope depositing their riders in the dirt. We heard more crashing of metal and shouting as the two following them ran smack into Vineet and Biker's bikes that were now lying flat on the trail, their wheels still spinning. We didn't hang around. If those hoodlums caught us now, they'd make mincemeat out of us. We splashed through the muddy pool at the bottom and rode desperately ahead thankful that the pursuit had at least temporarily ceased. We found Shiv and Pankaj waiting for us at the place where we had to lower our bikes into the gully in order to access the moat. Anshu had gone ahead with Khushboo and Salim.

'Oh my god!' Pankaj cried as he went up to Nasreen, who had been riding using just one arm and had turned very pale indeed. 'You've been hit!'

'I'm good, spiderman,' she whispered gamely. 'Let's move on.'

I wobbled along, beginning again to feel the burning sensation in my bum. I glanced back as best as I could. My jeans were ripped open and blood was running down the back of my thigh and leg. Immediately I felt dizzy. I felt Lavina's arm around my waist, steadying me.

'Easy, there, can you walk, Umi?' she asked gently. She smiled. 'Or should I pick you up and carry you?'

'I'll walk,' I said heroically.

Somehow we dragged our bikes up into the shelter of the step-well. Anshu took one look at me and shrieked, 'You're bleeding! Are you okay? What…?' She'd been too far ahead to know what had happened.

'I tripped them up but got shot I think,' I mumbled. 'Vineet shot me!'

'Oh my god!' She was all over me, hugging and kissing me and crying, as Lavina stroked my head. I glanced towards Nasreen. Pankaj was by her side, holding her hand and looking like he was going to cry, the dogs beside him, looking up anxiously. Khushboo and Salim looked like they were in shock; in a kind of coma almost.

'Come on, let's go to the den. We'll be safe there,' Anshu said, collecting herself and taking command again. 'Can you walk? Are you sure? Should we carry you?'

I nodded and then shook my head. 'I'll manage.' She gave me a whopper of a kiss and smiled, but her eyes were full of tears.

We held hands in a chain as we snaked through the tunnel, thankful that all of us had brought our torches. That walk through the tunnel was the longest walk I— and we—had ever done. By the end of it I could hardly hobble, my bum was on fire, and Lavina and Anshu were holding me up by the arms and almost dragging me on. Ahead of us poor Nasreen swayed dizzily from side to side, with Pankaj holding on to her grimly from one side. Shiv was now up front, holding on to Salim's hand the way you would hold the hand of someone who is blind. Khushboo staggered behind him like a zombie, clutching his hand. They were probably dimly wondering what the heck was happening and when they would wake up. The dogs were quietly bringing up the rear.

At last we reached the end of the tunnel and entered our shelter. We shut and bolted the doors firmly behind us: in the tunnel, thank god, we had heard no signs of pursuit. But Vineet and Biker would not give up so easily, they'd hang around, or maybe just go back home and wait for us there. Or god forbid, find the step-well and the tunnel entrance…It didn't bear thinking about.

Khushboo and Salim peered around through half-closed, swollen eyes.

'How did you find this place?' Khushboo whispered. 'Where are we?' Salim had not said a word. Probably he'd been hit on the head very hard with that cricket bat and the knuckleduster and was disoriented.

'We thought it would be a good hideout for you both,' Anshu said and shrugged. 'We didn't know that we'd have to use it so quickly.'

'Umi, take off your pants and lie face down on the bed,' Lavina suddenly barked at me, 'I want to have a look at your bottom.' I jolted awake. I'd been leaning against one of the cupboards as the others found seats and was beginning to feel rather woozy. Nasreen was sitting down still looking very pale and glancing at her arm. 'Nasreen, can you take off your top too, please?' Lavina went on, striding over to her and looking at her bloody arm. 'Looks like the bullet's grazed your shoulder. Anshu, help her. Pankaj, go get the first-aid box from the cupboard.' My sweet, gentle Lavina was in total command!

I went to the great 'four-poster' bed and turning bright red, took off my ripped jeans. I glanced down at my bum. It looked like a real mess! Feeling faint again, I lay down on my tummy.

'How're you feeling?' Lavina suddenly asked me peering at me and trying to smile. 'I had a good look at your bum, it's very cute but it's been gashed by the bullet. You may need a stitch or two.' She looked up. 'Shiv, get some gauze bandages and cotton-wool over here and dab the antiseptic.' She went off to where Nasreen was sitting in her chair, looking gaunter and gaunter.

'You have a gash too, Nasreen,' Lavina said, looking at Nasreen's slashed upper arm and shoulder. 'We need to dress it right away, put a pressure bandage on it—it's bleeding too much.' She looked up and then around the room and I could see that she was scared; her eyes had welled up and she was trying hard to stay in control and not to cry. Khushboo and Salim had sunk into the two armchairs and seemed more or less out of it: their eyes were nearly closed and they weren't registering much, glazed and unseeing. They must have been beaten pretty badly and the crazy bike ride afterwards would have traumatized them further. All of us really needed to be in a hospital. There was only so much poor Lavina and the others could do.

I was thinking again. Perhaps Shiv and Pankaj could sneak out and fetch help. In fact, they could be home in half an hour or so if they hurried. But there was always the danger that Vineet and Biker and Co. would be waiting for us to surface somewhere. Were they still searching for us on the Ridge and wondering where we had vanished? They didn't seem the type to give up easily. And they had had murder on their minds.

The dogs were now lying down peaceably watching us with their big eyes. They seemed to have suffered no ill-effects, though Lady-Bouncer still looked troubled. She was probably missing Badmash. Then suddenly, they all got to their feet and faced the door, their ears pricked.

'Ummph…the dogs,' Nasreen mumbled. She was

slumped in her armchair holding down a dressing to her wound hard to staunch the bleeding.

Dada suddenly barked and ran up to the door followed by Badi-Dadi and the rest. They sat down and whined, their tails wagging.

Had those psychos arrived at our doorstep?

Someone knocked firmly on the door and the handle turned. The door remained shut because we had locked it.

Then we heard a woman's voice from behind the door; a firm but worried sounding voice: 'Children? Will you please open up? Thank you!'

We stared at each other, our mouths dropping open. Silently Shiv went up to the door and then looked at all of us. We must have made quite a sight: Nasreen, her bloodstained blue top halfway down her body, holding on to one bloody arm with Pankaj hovering anxiously beside her; me with my bum bared for all to see, also slashed and bloody, with Anshu and Lavina hovering over it. And poor Khushboo and Salim looking like they'd just got off the zombie-express after it had fallen off a mountain cliff. Anshu nodded.

'Open the door,' she whispered.

Nasreen put her fingers in her mouth—ready to give her attack whistle, no doubt. Shiv unbolted the door and opened it and stood back. His jaw dropped.

Then he stood to attention and snapped a smart military salute. 'Ma'am!' he barked. 'Jai Hind!'

Of all the people on earth, the President of India in an elegant gold and green sari bustled in with a wriggling bug-eyed pug under her arm.

11

President Ayushi Khandelwal was a dumpy, bright-eyed little lady with a neat bun and a gentle, chubby face that 'babies would automatically smile at' as Anshu put it later. But it was known that she had a razor-sharp mind and tongue and didn't hold back in expressing herself. Politicians who had thought she was a harmless fuddy-duddy, good for promoting the image of women in the country and cuddling colicky babies, had lived to regret getting on her wrong side. And she was a crack computer-whiz and a surgeon, too!

'Children, are you all right? What happened to you all?' She fished out a maroon mobile and spoke snappily into it. 'The medicos are on their way.' The pug wriggled some more and tried to get down as the Six Pack (Five Pack now) whined at it eagerly and wagged their tails. The President looked at them.

'Can I put Golu down?' she asked. 'They won't eat

her?' Nasreen shook her head and then nodded, her eyes like grapefruit.

'Guys, she's a friend,' she told the pack, but the dogs already seemed to know that.

So I had been right! Pinpoint, GPS accurate! I'd figured out that the bomb-shelter indeed had been built directly under Rashtrapati Bhavan! The only mystery still to be solved was how had the President accessed the room, whereas we hadn't been able to find an access?

The answer was so simple we could have banged our heads against the wall. The entrance from Rashtrapati Bhavan was in the small hallway or lobby or whatever you'd like to call it between the two doors: the door leading from the tunnel outside and the door leading into the room proper. The one place where like idiots we had never bothered to look!

But now, I thought morosely, we could be in really deep trouble. We'd breached the President's security! The cops, or would it be the army or military police or some crack commando unit, were probably on their way charging down in their hob-nailed boots, automatic rifles and stun grenades at the ready. They'd take us to the dungeons of the Red Fort and torture us until we confessed to all sorts of things. Our parents would probably never see us again. There'd be all sorts of inquiries that would go on for months and months if not years.

For now, though, the President was at my bedside. And oh no, she was peering at my bloody, ripped-up bum. Can anything be more embarrassing than that? Then she looked from me to Lavina, standing next to me too (who had gone crimson) and her dark brown eyes twinkled amusedly, as she wagged a finger at us.

'Ah, so you're the lovey-dovey youngsters who came here yesterday! I watched you on the video feed and nearly came down here.' She glanced at the dogs. 'But your parents have trained your dogs very well,' she added dryly. Then she peered at my bum again. 'How on earth did that happen and how are you feeling? That's a rather nasty flesh wound. You've been shot, by the look of it. Thankfully, it doesn't seem serious but you need treatment, several stitches I would think! But first you'll have to tell us who shot at you.' She went over to poor Nasreen and gently examined her. 'Good heavens, child, you've been shot at too! What has been going on?' she said. Then she went over to Khushboo and Salim, still slumped in their armchairs, seemingly unaware that they were in the presence of the President of India. She flashed a torch into both of their eyes to check their pupils, I guess. 'Heavens, who did this to you all?' the President exclaimed, beginning to sound angry. 'You've both been beaten black and blue and you two are going into shock!' She looked at all of us.

'Children, what's going on? Who did this to you? Two of you have what I'm sure are bullet wounds and you two have been beaten to within an inch of your lives. You have all been assaulted brutally. Who did this to you?' Her eyes flashed angrily. 'And believe me they are going to pay! Now where the hell is that medical unit I asked for? The sooner we get you to hospital the better!' She started using her mobile again.

A lot of things began happening very fast immediately afterwards. A medical team, accompanied by a security detail armed to the teeth, turned up and 'secured' the place. We were stretchered up and taken to the swanky hospital on the premises of Rashtrapati Bhavan itself. The four of us who were injured were immediately tethered to IV lines. We all would remain here overnight, 'under observation'.

I lay on my tummy on what seemed to be an operating table as nurses rushed to and fro, and I could hear the murmur of conversation. Then a dumpy, masked and gowned figure came up to me, spectacles gleaming in the bright lights.

'How are you feeling, beta?'

I nodded. 'Okay, ma'am!' I whispered.

'Good, so now I'm going to put a few stitches to close up your injury, dear.'

I gasped.

The President of India was stitching up my bum!

Oh, god I thought nervously, please don't let me accidentally fart!

The President stitched me up real good as the nurses hovered around like flustered moths, probably wondering why the hell the Commander-in-Chief of the nation was doing this. She had already attended to Nasreen's arm. Khushboo and Salim's injuries were also dressed and attended to. They were in worse shape than us, suffering from concussion and shock besides all the bruising. The four who hadn't been hurt were also ordered to take 'bed-rest' by the doctor in charge.

Then the President sat at our bedside and heard out our story related to her by Anshu, from start to finish without interrupting: how Khushboo had been banned from seeing Salim and forcibly 'engaged' to Biker, the exchange of letters, the secret trysts in 'places of historical interest' that we had organized, culminating in the visit to Malcha Mahal. The President seemed pretty impressed.

'Remarkable, quite remarkable,' she said and then smiled. 'I suppose only teenagers could think of doing something like this.' Then Pankaj handed over his camera to her and as she saw the footage, her face went white and tight with anger. It was all there: Khushboo and Salim being dragged out of the Mahal by those psychos, those dreadful nooses and then Nasreen ordering the dogs to attack and the dogs pouncing.

After that there was a lot of jerky stuff as we fled on our cycles. But it was enough. The President beckoned one of the security fellows.

'See that these men are in custody in the next hour,' she snapped. Then she turned to Khushboo and Salim.

'My dear, how old are you?' she asked Khushboo.

'Ma'am, I'll be twenty-two tomorrow.' Khushboo replied, still looking dazed.

'And you are sure you wish to marry this young man?'

Khushboo nodded. 'Yes. I wish to marry him!'

'And you likewise want to marry her?' she asked Salim.

He nodded. 'Whenever she wants to, ma'am,' he said.

'We don't want to get married right away though, ma'am, but at some point definitely. We've known each other since we were children…'

'Then you shall get married. And you will be married here at Rashtrapati Bhavan as my personal guests, if you so wish, whenever you choose to! It's time certain political elements in this country are taught a lesson.' There was pure steel in her voice.

Khushboo and Salim just looked speechlessly at each other and then at the President.

'Thank you, ma'am, so much,' Khushboo whispered.

It was kind of unbelievable and I could see that Shiv

had become a total fanboy. Of course, the President had to keep snubbing and snapping at her security and bodyguards who had really got their jodhpurs in a twist at our seemingly appalling transgression of top-secret security and kept trying to question us, muttering 'protocol, protocol', to which the President snapped, 'file it!' Imagine! A bunch of shot-up, beaten-up young people had turned up right inside the hallowed premises of the President of India's home with zero security clearance. It was unheard of!

They called up and personally fetched our shocked parents, who first thought we were playing some crazy prank on them, until the shiny black limos with Presidential number plates screeched up at our complex, escorted by police cars and a lot of huffing and puffing policemen. Khushboo's parents were taken into custody for questioning too.

Vineet and Biker and Co. were quickly rounded up: they'd gone back home, attended to their dog bites and other injuries and incandescent with rage, had been waiting to ambush Anshu and me under our stairwell. The police had found poor Raghav (who turned out to be Khushboo and Vineet's nephew) too, gagged and bound and terrified in Biker's garage. After being forcibly made to spy on and betray us, Vineet and Biker had decided that he couldn't be trusted to keep his mouth shut.

Raghav had indeed spotted Khushboo's love letter lying at the bottom of my bag when he was looking for the first-aid kit the day I got injured during cricket coaching. And with 'To my dearest darling Salim, from your sweetest Khushboo' inscribed all over the front of the envelope, you didn't have to be a crack detective to know what was going on! Vineet and Biker had been strong-arming poor Raghav right from the start, terrorizing and threatening him to do their bidding and hitting him around to show they were serious. That's why he was always covered in those mysterious bruises. Bullied and beaten by his cousin, he had naturally told Vineet about the letter. But soon after, he realized the enormity of what he had done: virtually sentenced Khushboo and Salim to their deaths! Vineet and Biker had taken one look at Raghav, who was on the verge of panicking, and decided to get rid of him after they'd taken care of the others.

Anshu and I for one had certainly underestimated Vineet. Obviously, he hadn't really trusted us at all and had suspected us of being 'double-agents'.

It turned out that the secret bomb-shelter *had* been built during World War II to protect the Viceroy and his family and everyone had indeed forgotten all about it after the War had ended.

As she sat by our bedside, the President told us her part of the story.

'Well, you see my dears, I don't get very much time to myself and when I do, I usually disappear into a little secret reading room that I had discovered, with Golu. One morning, Golu got very excited and went and sat beside a large bookshelf, cocking her head this way and that and whining. Well, I thought maybe a rat had got caught behind the books, so began emptying the shelves. There I discovered the little vent through which, to my astonishment, I heard the voices of children! You children! I decided to investigate further without informing anyone else. So I lowered a tiny microphone and video camera down the vent.' She looked a bit embarrassed. 'I began eavesdropping on you and monitoring you. Of course, I was not there most of the time so the mic was voice-activated and the camera transmitted audio and video feed directly to my phone.'

'Wow, ma'am!' Shiv said, his eyes shining.

She smiled. 'You play the guitar very well, my dear,' she told Anshu. 'And I can't tell you how impressed I was by what you said the other day about religion and politics. I'm going to arrange for recordings of that to be sent to every Member of Parliament and political leader, and of course the media with the message that this is what the children of India have told me in confidence.' She smiled at us. 'I was really expecting you children to get up to mischief, but I have to say that children like you, and what you have done for those two lovely youngsters make me so proud of this country.'

We tried to look modest (Anshu was glowing like a hi-powered LED bulb) as she went on with her story.

'But like you I was wondering about the entrance to the bomb-shelter from here and then figured that if the vent was hidden behind the bookshelf, maybe there was a door here too. And sure enough I found it. The whole bookshelf swings open like the heavy door of a safe and there's another door behind it! So just the other day I opened the door and ventured down the stairs and...we, Golu and I, found the shelter! I installed a couple of motion sensing wireless baby cams. They're on the top of the cupboards for a clearer HD picture.' She looked a little sheepish again.

'I was sure I'd catch you smoking or indulging in other unsavoury activities involving syringes but you didn't, so I really had no reason to crash your party!'

'No problem, ma'am,' Shiv said.

She glanced at me and Lavina and smiled. 'I knew at once why you two had come down here alone yesterday and was wondering whether I'd have to intervene but your sweet dogs took care of that problem.'

Both Lavina and I went absolutely beetroot. Imagine being confronted by the President of India while in the throes of passionately making out!

Her face grew serious. 'Until, of course, this evening,

when you turned up looking like you'd emerged from the trenches of World War I.'

We told her about Badmash and she immediately sent a team out to Malcha Mahal to check. They found the poor fellow limping along Sardar Patel Road, on his way home. He'd been winged in a hind leg, but would be fine and was delighted to rejoin the pack.

We stayed on as guests of the President for two whole days till she was sure we were fit to go back home, much to the horror of her security detail. We were shown around Rashtrapati Bhavan by members of the staff and her ADCs and whatnot as if we were VVIPs, which was totally awesome. 'The place really needs a gang of kids to create some halla and make it seem like a normal home,' the President told us, her eyes twinkling. 'Everything here is so stiff and starched with protocol, it's unbelievable!' Needless to say, they sealed up the tunnel entrance at the step-well and we can no longer access the bomb-shelter from it. There were plans to actually block the tunnel solid to ensure that no such security breach could ever take place again. We didn't mind too much. The President had given us a secret telephone number so we could access the bomb-shelter from the private reading room. We just had to call up, and a member of the staff would be at one of the gates (I cannot divulge which) to escort us inside—after we had proven our identity, of course.

But it did sort of lose its charm and we never used it.

Still, the step-well was still pretty much our private little swimming pool because after it had been thoroughly checked out by security (for what, we had no idea) it was equally promptly forgotten by everyone.

Just two days after we had gone back home, we received a summons from Rashtrapati Bhavan. All we were told was that the President had requested our company for a press conference she was holding. The Presidential limos picked us up and when we reached, we were stunned to see the amount of security in place. Commandos strutted around everywhere wielding murderous automatic guns and we were thoroughly frisked. As we were hustled into the green room to be 'made up' for the cameras, we heard sirens and everyone started scurrying around. Then the President entered the room, along with Khushboo and Salim, who were also looking quite dazed, and smiled at us.

'You must be wondering what this is all about,' she started. 'Well, I am going to address the nation and tell them about what happened. This will be telecast live all over the country. I have personally invited the Prime Minister and Home Minister and Leader of the Opposition to attend too. Oh, that's probably them arriving just now.' There was a steely glint in the lady's eyes.

We were shown our seats on the dais and looked

around bemused. The place was jammed with media. The seating arrangement was simple: the President sat in the middle, flanked by the Prime Minister and Home Minister on either side of her (looking uncomfortable), the Leader of the Opposition was beside the Home Minister and Khushboo and Salim in turn flanking the politicians, both now looking quite nervous. We were equally distributed on either side of them. Behind us, hawk-eyed Black Cat Commandos scanned the crowd.

The national anthem was played and then the President began her address. In a level, firm tone she described what had happened with Khushboo and Salim and our role in helping them out. The video that Pankaj had made at Malcha Mahal was shown.

'I am sorry and ashamed to say that this is what we seem to have achieved as a people after so many years of Independence—and all of you, watching this at home and here in this studio, ought to be sorry and ashamed too,' the President concluded. 'It took the courage and kindness of these children, two of whom were shot at, to save this couple. Since when have we become a people who shoot our children and try to hang those who love each other? Is this something we ought to be proud of? Is this something religions teach us?' She paused and then smiled. 'But I am happy to say that at least our children have shown wisdom and courage in this matter. It gives me hope for the future.'

Lavina leaned across to me. 'Umi, she's sounding like a schoolteacher now,' she whispered. I remained poker faced. But our President had not finished and now delivered her coup-de-grace. She glanced balefully at the Prime Minister and Home Minster, both shifting uncomfortably in their seats.

'As you have been informed, I will personally oversee the arrangements of Khushboo and Salim's wedding and it will be done in my presence. You gentlemen have been cordially invited and will be obliged to attend.' Her voice became steely. 'If anyone, absolutely anyone, dares lift a finger against them at any time, or trolls them in any manner, we shall find them and I shall be holding those in office personally responsible! Is that clear?'

Man, were we stunned! The Prime Minister and Home Minster looked as if they had been solidly punched in the kidneys. She had made everything clear in front of the entire nation. What a lady!

'Does she have guts or what,' Lavina said, shock and awe in her voice. I nodded. 'Those fellows look like schoolboys who have been told to stand in the corner!'

Again, hard though it was, I remained poker faced.

For the media of course, this was a story to end all stories and for days they hounded us. It stopped when we put the Six Pack in charge of our own security. But millions of young people all around the country had streamed into the streets and public spaces and vociferously cheered our President.

Eventually, Khushboo and Salim did get married, quietly. We were all invited, as well as Salim's delighted family. They were given accommodation by the President until the press, and probably everyone else, lost interest in them. No one dared raise a finger against them. Obviously, strict orders had been issued from the very top (the Prime Minister's office no doubt), that the couple were to be left alone and there would be hell if anyone tried anything. Khushboo now teaches (and does research in) History and English Literature at Jawaharlal Nehru University, and Salim is training to become a surgeon. They've moved to their own place, the address of which I cannot divulge.

We all met at the step-well again, very soon afterwards. Both Nasreen's and my dressings had just been removed and Khushboo and Salim too had recovered well. I sneaked down a few steps of the well and positioned myself in a beam of sunlight. I looked around. The others appeared to have gone down to the water. I lowered my trunks and surreptitiously sneaked a peek at my bum.

'What are you doing?' Lavina suddenly asked, materializing out of the gloom and making me jump.

Then she dissolved into giggles. 'Are you admiring your scar?' She was looking at my bum and giggling now uncontrollably.

'Just wanted to see how big it is,' I muttered quickly hitching up my trunks. 'She said she had to put in forty-six stitches!'

'Here,' she said helpfully producing a small hand-mirror. 'Use this. But I can tell you she's done a marvellous job. It's just like fine embroidery.' This was followed by another paroxysm of giggles.

'Eh? What? Why are you giggling like that?'

'See for yourself!'

Without thinking I lowered my trunks again and peered at the reflection in the mirror she was holding out to me. She had been right.

Not only did it look like embroidery, it stretched right across one cheek of my bum, like a slightly drunken, but very happy smiley! And there was what looked suspiciously like a dimple at one end of the smiley.

'I always knew you were cute,' Lavina giggled, 'but with a dimple and a smiley stretched across your bum: well, you're irresistible! How many girls can boast of having boyfriends who have that?'

She patted it gently and then took me in her arms and kissed me.

www.ingramcontent.com/pod-product-compliance
Lightning Source LLC
Chambersburg PA
CBHW061522050726
47503CB00015B/2580